Carol

(*Original Title:* Carol from the Country)

by FRIEDA FRIEDMAN

Illustrated by MARY BARTON

SCHOLASTIC  BOOK SERVICES

Published by Scholastic Book Services, a division
of Scholastic Magazines, Inc., New York, N. Y.

* By the same author

A SUNDAE WITH JUDY
DOT FOR SHORT
JANITOR'S GIRL

* also available from Scholastic Book Services

Single copy price 45¢. Quantity prices available on request.

 This Scholastic Book Services edition is published by arrangement with William Morrow & Company, Inc.

1st printing .... April 1966

Printed in the U.S.A.

Contents

1. Carol from the Country 1
2. Carol Has Callers 13
3. A Letter from Helen 30
4. The Contest 44
5. Carol Gets Busy 57
6. A Visit to the Library 70
7. The Prize 81
8. Where Are the Twins? 95
9. The Search 106
10. Miss Tyler Doesn't Knock 122
11. Carol's Friends 136

Chapter I

Carol from the Country

NEVER, not once in her eleven and a half years, had Carol felt as unhappy as she did today, the first day in the new apartment. As she helped Mother get things in order, Carol kept very quiet. She was afraid that if she spoke, her voice would quaver and she might even burst out crying. She was afraid she would say something angry and impolite. Over and over again she told herself that Mother and Daddy should have found a way for the family to continue to live in the country. They should have figured out a better plan, so that Carol and the others did not have to move into this small, hot apartment on a noisy, crowded street in noisy, crowded New York.

Mother and the twins, Jinny and Johnny, chatted and laughed as gaily as if nothing terrible had happened. How could they? The twins were young, of course — only eight and a half — so they didn't understand; but what about Mother, who had always been so proud of her lovely home?

Unlike Mother and the twins, Daddy was always quiet, and now he was even quieter than usual. After supper was over and the dishes had been put away, Daddy said he was going to give an order that must be obeyed. Everyone looked up at him in surprise, for Daddy hardly ever gave orders.

"I order all of the Clarks to sit down and rest, and not do another bit of work today," he said. "We're all hot and tired, and it's been quite a day."

Mother obeyed immediately. She sighed as she dropped into the big armchair that looked bigger than ever in the tiny living room. "It certainly has been quite a day," she said, mopping the perspiration from her forehead just below her curly brown hair. "Moving's no fun on a hot July day."

"Moving's no fun on any day," Carol thought angrily. "Not when you move out of a nice big house and away from all your friends. I'd never invite the girls to a place like this."

She looked around the living room, and it seemed

to her that the four walls were closer than ever. And the apartment was so hot. Not a breeze came through the open window. How could it with tall buildings on both sides and across the street?

The twins did not agree with Mother. "Moving is fun! It's loads of fun," shouted Jinny, whose real name was Virginia. She had hardly finished her sentence when Johnny added his opinion. "Nothing's as much fun as moving into a new city and meeting new kids." In spite of the heat, he and Jinny bounced up and down as they talked. Their eyes, large and gray like Mother's, danced with excitement. Mother grinned at them, and the worried look disappeared for a while from Daddy's thin, serious face.

Carol wanted to shake her brother and sister for being so silly. Imagine wanting to meet the boys and girls who lived on a street like this! Carol pressed her lips together. She took a few steps to the bookcase and took out a new book. It was the one that her best friend, Helen, had given her for a going-away present. She read the words Helen had written on the front page: "To my best friend, Carol. I will never forget you." Tears filled Carol's eyes. She turned around quickly and looked outside before the others noticed.

Across the street was a row of five-story buildings, all exactly alike, all dirty gray in color. They all had fire escapes going down from the top floor to the first. The fire escapes looked like ugly iron porches connected by iron steps. How different they were from the lovely white porch on the house in the country! On the ground floor of every building across the street there was a store. Carol could see a candy store, a vegetable store, a butcher shop, and a radio store. On the sidewalk in front of the vegetable store were husks of corn and some old lettuce leaves. A scattered newspaper lay in the gutter.

"How ugly everything is," Carol thought. She wondered if she would ever again see a tree or a garden or even a little blade of green grass. She wondered if she would ever go back to visit her friends. If she did, she would have to invite them here. Again Carol told herself that she would never, never do that.

Carol decided it would be better to read than to stand looking out and thinking about how unhappy she was. She sat in the chair next to the window and started to read Helen's book. Through the open fourth-floor window came so many disagreeable sounds that she hardly knew what she was reading. She heard the repeated honking of automobile horns, the deep rumbling of a bus that passed the door, the squeal of auto brakes, loud band music coming from one nearby radio and a loud speech coming from another. She heard the shouts of children playing in the street. "Get the ball! Get the ball!" they yelled. Was it ever quiet enough to read in New York, Carol wondered.

As if the sounds from outside were not enough, there was a sudden loud crash from upstairs. It shook the ceiling. Carol looked up to see if the chandelier was still there. It was, but it was shaking a little. The crash was followed by the shrill screaming of a baby. Carol bit her lip in disgust. It was bad enough to have so much noise outside, but it was even worse to have a noisy family right overhead. "I hate New York," she told herself bitterly. "And I know I'll hate everyone in it, too."

Noise never bothered Jinny and Johnny. They looked at the ceiling for a second, then went right on talking. "I wish it was tomorrow already," Johnny said, "so we could go outside and meet all the kids on this street." He jumped high in the air as he said it and came down on the floor with a bang. Jinny tried to jump even higher. "Me too, me too!" she shouted. "I wish it was tomorrow today." They jumped up and down like two jack-in-the-boxes.

At that moment there was another noise. This time it came from downstairs. It was a loud, sharp tap, tap, tap, as if someone below were knocking on the ceiling.

Mother and Daddy looked at each other in a questioning way. "I'm afraid that's our neighbor downstairs telling us to be more quiet," Daddy explained. "They knock on the ceiling in New York when there's too much noise, or they bang on the radiator pipes."

"We didn't knock when those people upstairs almost broke down our ceiling," Carol said angrily. Now she felt herself disliking the people downstairs as much as she did those upstairs. She knew she would dislike the families in the apartments on both sides, too. That was another trouble with living in New York. There were people upstairs, downstairs, to the left, to the right. She could even hear a click when someone turned on the electric light next door. "This isn't a home at all," she thought. "If only we could go back to the country!"

If the twins had changed the subject, Carol would have gone to bed that night without losing her temper or saying out loud any of the angry things she told herself. But when Johnny and Jinny liked a subject, they liked to go on talking about it.

Now Jinny turned to Carol. "Don't you think living in New York is going to be fun?" she asked.

It was more than Carol could stand. She didn't mind keeping quiet, but she was not going to tell a lie. She snapped the book shut. Her dark-blue eyes flashed and filled with angry tears. "No, I don't think it's going to be fun at all," she said sharply. "I think New York is terrible. I think this apartment is ugly and the street is awful and the people are sure to be . . ."

"Carol!" Mother's voice stopped her. Never had it sounded so stern, so really angry. Never had Mother's merry gray eyes looked so serious. Carol knew that Mother wanted to shake her for hurting Daddy's feelings. All that Mother thought about these days was Daddy's feelings. Why didn't she care how Carol felt? There didn't seem to be any use talking. Carol put the book back into the bookcase.

"I think I'll take a bath and go to bed," she said, without looking directly at anyone. Her voice sounded very tired.

"That's a good idea," Daddy told her gently. "You've done a lot of work today, honey, and you've been a big help. Get a good night's sleep."

In the small bedroom, Carol sat down for a minute and looked around her. This room, which she and Jinny would have to share from tonight on, was about one third the size of the room that had been her very own back home. The double bed, the dresser, and the one chair took up so much room that you could hardly walk around. And the noise! Like the living room, the bedroom faced the street, and Carol could hear all the street noises as well as the hum of an airplane that must be flying low. Above the noise of the auto horns and brakes, the rumbling of buses, the loud voices coming from radios all around, and the shouts of children, came an even louder sound. It was a woman's voice, and it came from the window directly over Carol's.

"Pat, you come right upstairs and take your bath," the voice yelled. "The kids took theirs and now it's your turn. You hear me?" Carol decided that Pat must be very deaf if he didn't hear.

Pat evidently heard, for a very loud voice, this time a boy's, boomed up past Carol's window. "Aw, Ma, give me ten minutes more, will you, Ma?" Carol decided then and there that Pat was the kind of boy she would never like; nor would she ever like anyone in his noisy family.

Carol passed by the mirror over the bureau and looked at herself. The girl in the mirror was tall for her age, and slim. Like Daddy, she had a thin, serious face, dark-blue eyes, and blond hair. Her hair was shoulder length, and it curled at the ends. Carol studied herself in the mirror. "No one will ever know I have a dimple," she thought, "because it only shows when I smile, and I'll never have anything to smile at in New York." She forced herself to smile, just to be sure that the dimple was still there.

The bathtub was old and scratched. Even after Carol scrubbed it, it looked dirty. This room was very different from the big bathroom at home with its stall shower. Carol didn't try to hide her tears now, as she thought of the house they had all lived in until . . . was it only this morning? It had been such a pretty house, with a porch in front, a garden in the back, and grass on all sides. The rooms had been large and sunny. No one else lived upstairs or downstairs, and even on hot days like this there was a breeze. You could hear the birds singing in the morning — a much pleasanter sound than any of the noises Carol had heard today.

As she returned to her bedroom across the long, narrow hall, she heard Daddy's voice saying, "Pleasant dreams, honey." She tried to make her "Good night" sound natural. It hurt her to be angry at Daddy, for she and Daddy had always been such good friends. People said that they looked alike and were alike in many ways. And Daddy had never failed Carol except this once.

Carol remembered how serious Mother had looked one day last month when she told Carol and the twins the bad news. Daddy must sell his shoe store and they would all have to move to New York, where he had been offered a position in someone else's shoe store. "This is very hard on your father," Mother had said. "It's harder on him than on you, because he wanted you three children to have everything in the world. Help him all you can, won't you?"

Even then the twins had been as excited as if Mother had told them good news. To Carol, the news had been such a shock that she didn't know what to say. The thought of leaving her friends, her school, and the town she had been born in made her feel sad even then. And at that time she had not known the kind of apartment they would move into.

Carol pretended to be asleep when she heard Jinny come into the room. Jinny clicked on the electric light and started to talk. "Golly," she said, "I can't wait till tomorrow to meet all the new kids. And I can't wait to go to the Central Park Zoo and see all the animals. Golly, moving's fun!"

Jinny turned out the light, jumped into bed, and

soon fell asleep. Carol turned from side to side, wide awake. She didn't want to make new friends. She wanted to be back with the old ones. It wouldn't be fair to Helen to make new friends. And anyway, New York people couldn't be as nice as the ones back home. Carol didn't see how she could ever be happy again.

Chapter 2

Carol Has Callers

CAROL was awake early the next morning, but instead of opening her eyes, she buried her face in her pillow. "Maybe when I look up I'll find myself home in my own bedroom," she told herself. "Maybe the moving was all a dream. Maybe . . ."

The loud ring of the telephone interrupted Carol's thoughts. It rang shrilly a few times, stopped for a while, then began to ring again. Carol wondered why Mother didn't answer. There! The ringing had stopped. With her eyes still closed, Carol waited eagerly to hear what Mother would say.

"Hello, you wish to speak to Maria? Why, of course!" said a pleasant voice with a foreign accent. Carol sat up in bed quickly. Who in the world was

Maria, and who was it out there with a foreign accent?

Someone else began to talk. This person had an accent too, but not such a noticeable one. Fully awake now, Carol understood. It wasn't the Clarks' telephone that had rung. The Clarks could not afford to have a telephone. The voice Carol heard came from the other side of the bedroom wall, from a room so close that Carol could hear every word.

No, the moving to New York was not a dream.

The bed began to bounce as Jinny jumped out. "Let's get going right away," she said. "We've got all those new people to meet today." When Carol did not move, Jinny looked hard at her. "You're coming, aren't you?" she asked.

Carol pretended that she was considering it. No, she told Jinny, there was still so much to do in the house that she'd better stay home and help Mother. She started to get out of bed.

Jinny turned up her small, freckled nose and shook her head in an understanding way. "You're an old stuck-up, that's what you are," she told her sister. "You think these kids aren't good enough for you." She poked her curly head out of the door and screamed down the hall, "Hey, Johnny, Miss Stuck-up isn't coming downstairs with us."

"Who cares?" Johnny called back.

Mother had eaten her breakfast earlier with Daddy, but she sat down at the table with Carol and the twins. As they were eating their cereal, a bell rang. They all looked at one another. Nobody moved.

The bell rang again. This time Mother got up. "I'll press this button. It opens the downstairs door. Jinny, you open the hall door and see who it is."

Mother pushed a button in the wall. They all heard a tick-tick-ticking sound. Jinny opened the door into the hall and waited. "No one's here, and no one's coming upstairs," she called back.

The bell rang again, once, twice, three times, as if someone were getting impatient.

Johnny's eyes sparkled. He jumped up excitedly. "I know! It's the dumb-waiter!" he announced.

"That's just it!" Mother answered. "Mr. Swensen told us yesterday that he collects the garbage every morning." Mother, followed closely by Jinny and Johnny, opened a door that was built into one of the kitchen walls. Carol left her cereal and followed. Neither she nor any of the Clarks had ever seen a dumb-waiter.

When Mother opened the door, they saw a brick wall opposite them and two ropes, one near them and another back of it. There did not seem to be anything to put the garbage pail on.

"Where do I put the garbage?" Mother called down. They all heard a hearty laugh from down in the basement. "You put it on the dumb-waiter shelf, but I guess I haven't got it high enough for you," said Mr. Swensen, the janitor. The ropes began to move. Very soon a wooden shelf with a pail and wastepaper basket appeared on a level with the Clarks' dumb-waiter door. The ropes continued to move and the shelf rose still higher. Now Carol saw that there was a lower shelf too, and a third rope held them in place. Mother put the garbage pail, and

a box full of crumpled newspapers from the unpacking, on the empty lower shelf.

"All right," she called down. Now the ropes began to move again and the dumb-waiter went down, down, down till it was in the basement, where Mr. Swenson could remove the garbage and trash.

A few minutes later the bell rang again. Again Mother opened the dumb-waiter door. Carol, right behind her, saw the ropes moving and the shelves rising till the lower one was level with the door.

"Is it okay?" asked a girl's voice.

"Fine, thanks," Mother answered. "Is this Mrs. Swensen?" There was no way of seeing who was in the basement when you looked down the dumb-waiter shaft.

"No, I'm Christine. I'm helping Daddy with the garbage," said the girl's voice.

"Yippee, I wish I was her," Johnny said. "I'd love to pull those ropes from the basement to the top. And I'd love to stand on the top shelf and get a ride. Maybe some day I will."

Carol was disgusted. "That dumb-waiter was dusty," she reminded Johnny, "and the shelves don't look clean. Some of the garbage must have spilled over. I'd hate to be that Christine."

Mother said that in many of the tall New York

apartment houses dumb-waiters were used to save climbing the stairs. "That's how groceries and other packages are delivered. Otherwise errand boys would often have to climb up five flights with heavy parcels."

After breakfast, the twins rushed out of the house to meet their new friends. Mother and Carol began to put away the dishes. The company dishes, which were not used often, would go on the top shelf of the kitchen cabinet. Mother stood on a ladder, and Carol dusted the plates and handed them to her a few at a time.

While they were doing this, a bell rang again. Carol put down the dishes and opened the dumb-waiter door. "Yes?" she called. There was no answer. Mother suggested that she try the door to the hall.

Carol wished she were the one on the ladder, so that Mother would have to open the door. Who could it possibly be?

A girl about Carol's own age stood at the door. She was a little shorter than Carol and much plumper. She had bushy black hair and smiling gray eyes. Carol noticed immediately that her dress was too short and too tight, and not at all the right style for such a plump girl. She did have a friendly smile, though.

"I'm Ruth Silverman," the girl introduced herself. "Mind if I come in, Carol?"

Carol wondered how the girl knew her name. She led Ruth into the kitchen and introduced her to Mother. Mother came down from the ladder, told the visitor to sit down, and said that it was very nice of her to pay the Clarks a visit.

Again Ruth smiled her broad, friendly smile. "To tell you the truth, I didn't think of it by myself," she explained. "I met the twins outside, and they introduced themselves. They're the cutest kids." Ruth looked at Mother. "They look like you," she said. Mother's smile showed how pleased she was. "Well, they told me to come upstairs and introduce myself to Carol, because she's too shy to go out and make friends. So here I am."

Carol almost gasped out loud. Those brats! She was so angry at the twins that she could feel her face getting red. It made her even angrier to see that Mother's eyes looked as if she were amused. She was biting her lower lip to keep from smiling.

After visiting for about ten minutes and telling Carol all about the teacher she would probably have in September, Ruth said good-bye. "See you in the park tomorrow, if I don't see you before," were her farewell words.

Mother, still smiling, climbed up on the ladder

again. "What a nice, friendly girl," she said. "And did you notice her smile?"

"Did you notice how tight her dress was?" Carol asked, without answering Mother's question. "When people outgrow their clothes, why don't they give them away or throw them away or something?"

Mother said it was probably because the people did not have enough money for a new dress, and a short, tight dress was better than none at all. Carol looked down at the hem of the blue cotton dress she was wearing. It was a big hem, thank goodness, so next year it wouldn't look skimpy, as Ruth Silverman's dress did.

About five minutes later the doorbell rang again. This time the ring was loud and long. When Carol opened the door, she saw a tall boy about thirteen years old standing outside. He had the reddest sunburn, the reddest hair, and the reddest freckles that Carol had ever seen. There was not an inch of his round face that was not covered with freckles. His eyes were brown. He wore a bright green shirt and he chewed bubble gum loudly.

"Hi! I'm Pat Daly," he said, walking past Carol into the living room. "I live upstairs. The twins told me you're too bashful to make friends. That's what I call plain dumb." Pat made a big bubble with his gum, snapped it loudly, and grinned. Carol was thoroughly disgusted. She had been sure last night, when she heard Pat's loud voice, that she would not like him. She had been right. She did not like his voice, his manners, or his bright green shirt.

Pat walked around the room, looking at everything. "It sure looks better now," he said. "Nice furniture," he added, touching the sofa. "And a piano. Gosh, you must be rich!" He sat on the piano bench, pressed the loud pedal down as far as it would go, and began to play "Chopsticks." Carol just stood there, wondering what to do. In the middle of Pat's playing there was a thump-thump-thump on the floor. Instead of stopping, Pat put all ten fingers on the keys and played a loud, terrible-sounding chord. Then he stopped.

By now Mother was in the living room, and before Carol could introduce Pat he introduced himself. "We used to live here," he said, to the surprise of Carol and her mother. "But Mrs. Pain-in-the-neck was always knocking, so when the place upstairs was empty we moved in. Say, you're not the kind of people who knock, are you?"

"Is that really her name, Mrs. Pain-in . . . What did you say it was?" Carol asked.

Pat threw back his red, curly head and laughed so hard that he swallowed his gum. Then he began to cough. Carol did not know what she had said that was so funny. She did not like being laughed at, and now she disliked Pat more than ever.

When he stopped coughing and laughing, Pat explained that the kids called her Mrs. Pain-in-the-neck because she was so grouchy. Her real name was Miss Tyler. She lived all alone. She did not like children or anyone else. Most of all she did not like noise.

Mother began to look worried as Pat talked. "I'm afraid you'll have to move up another floor and let us take your apartment," she said jokingly to Pat. "The twins make a lot of noise."

Pat said that he lived on the top floor now, and one more move would be to the roof. He and Mother laughed like old friends. Again Carol wondered about Mother. Didn't she care where she lived or what kind of friends she had? Why, she seemed really to like Pat.

Pat visited for a few minutes more, ate some chocolate cookies that Mother brought out, then said good-bye. "Be seeing you in the park tomorrow, Carrie," he said.

Carol drew herself up tall and held her head high.

"Carol, not Carrie," she corrected him. She had never liked the nickname Carrie and never let anyone call her by it. Back home, Helen's brother Bill had called her Carrie once in a while, just to tease her and see how angry she would get.

"Well, I hope that's the end of the visitors for today," she said as she helped Mother make the beds. "I can't say that I really liked either of them."

"Is that so?" Mother said, looking surprised. "I thought they were both nice and friendly."

As she put on the bedspread, Carol stepped back and bumped into the wall. What a tiny room, she thought. There wasn't any space to move around in. Imagine Pat thinking that the Clarks must be rich. She remembered the patch in his trouser leg and realized that the Dalys must be very poor.

When the doorbell rang again a short time later, Carol wished she could pretend that she was not home. She knew just what the visitor would say. He or she would say, "I met the twins and they said you're too shy to make friends, so I thought I'd visit you."

Outside the door this time there were three people, one boy and two girls. One girl was tall and slim, with very dark skin and dark eyes. Her black hair hung loose across her shoulders. It was so uneven that Carol knew her mother must have cut it, or maybe she cut her own hair. The boy looked like her. He too was dark, with dark eyes and dark hair.

The other girl looked different from any of the girls Carol had seen in the neighborhood. She was small and very pretty. She had short, light-brown curly hair, brown eyes, and pink cheeks. It was not her looks, though, as much as her clothes that attracted Carol. The girl wore a beautiful plaid cotton dress with crisp white cuffs that looked as if they had just been pressed.

"I wouldn't mind knowing her," Carol found herself thinking.

The small girl seemed to be the leader. "Hello, Carol. I'm Elizabeth Warren, but everyone calls me Betsy," she said. "This is Maria Zeccino and this is her cousin, Frank. The twins told us to come up and visit you."

Well, at least Betsy did not mention anything about shyness. Carol liked her all the better for that.

They followed Carol into the living room, where Mother joined them. When Maria said, "I am so glad to meet you," to Mother, something about her soft, pleasant voice with its slight accent seemed familiar to Carol. Why, it was the voice she had heard talking on the telephone this morning. Maria must live right next door.

Then Carol found herself clenching her fist as she

listened to Maria telling what the twins had said. Betsy looked at Maria as if she wanted to stop her, but Maria went on and on. She turned to Carol. "Lots of people are shy. It doesn't really matter," she said.

Carol found herself flushing angrily. Shyness had nothing to do with it. She just did not want to know New York people, girls whose dresses were too short and tight, whose hair was cut badly, and who had accents. She didn't want to know boys who wore bright green shirts. Betsy was different. If only she could separate Betsy from the others and make Betsy her best friend in New York! Helen would always be her very, very best friend, of course.

Carol realized that she had missed part of the conversation. Maria was explaining that Frank was quiet because he was not sure of his English. "He and his mama and papa live with us right next door, and his papa helps my papa in the shoe-repair shop downstairs." Maria paused to catch her breath. Maybe Frank did not like to talk, but Maria certainly did. "My family has been in this country five years," she boasted. "Frankie came from Italy only five months ago, so he is not yet an American."

When Maria said that, Frankie's dark, serious eyes flashed. He whirled toward his cousin. "I *am*

American," he said in a voice that trembled with anger. "Now I am not in Italy, no? Now I am here. I *am* American. Why you say not?"

Betsy came to the rescue. "Of course you are," she said gently. "You're as good an American as any of us. Maria didn't really mean it."

Frank looked less angry as he listened to Betsy. Carol could tell that he liked her. "She shouldn't talk so," he said. "She talks too much." Everyone laughed.

To change the subject, Mother asked Betsy if her father was the Doctor Warren whose sign was on the corner building. Betsy said that he was and that he was the very best doctor in the world. Again Carol found herself thinking that she wanted Betsy to be her friend. She could not picture herself writing to Helen and saying that her best friend in New York was the daughter of a man who had a shoe-repair shop. But a doctor's daughter! That sounded very nice.

When they were all at the door saying good-bye, Betsy said, "Be sure to be at the park tomorrow." Then they all rushed down the four flights of stairs before Carol could ask them what would be happening at the park. Not that she cared, for she certainly was not going there.

When the bell rang again at noon, Carol and Mother did not look at each other questioningly. They knew by the banging on the door and the rattling of the doorknob that it must be the twins. Then a key turned in the door and Daddy marched down the hall with Jinny behind him and Johnny behind her, as if they were part of a parade. They marched into the kitchen, where Mother and Carol were setting the table.

"We went to the store and waited for Daddy to come home for lunch with us," Jinny explained. "Everyone in the store seemed to like us."

"Everyone in the whole street did," Johnny added. "We musta made about fifty new friends this morning, and we're not finished yet. Anything happen here?" He looked at Jinny as he asked. She winked at him.

"We made friends too." Mother answered before Carol could say anything. "We had visitors, two boys and three girls, and they were just as nice as could be." Mother turned to Daddy. "How was everything in the store, dear?" she asked.

Daddy said it was always hard to make a change and start something new, but he was sure he would get used to the new store in time. "We all get used to things after a while," he said, and although he looked directly at Mother, Carol knew that he was talking to her.

They were seated around the table now, and the table was close to the window, so that they would be as cool as possible. From where she was sitting Carol could see the courtyard with the tall poles, and with clotheslines running from one pole to another. On the clotheslines were all kinds of things: underwear, handkerchiefs, children's sun suits, big sheets — some with holes in them — towels, ladies' slips, and summer dresses. They all belonged to people Carol did not know or care about. Up until yesterday, when Carol had looked out of the kitchen window, she had seen a garden. No, Daddy was wrong. She would never, never get used to this.

Chapter 3

A Letter from Helen

IT SEEMED to Carol that in all her eleven and a half years she had not heard as many bells ring as during these two days in New York. There were the upstairs bell, the downstairs bell, and the dumb-waiter bell. Each one sounded a little different. One rang now.

"That's the downstairs bell," Jinny announced proudly. "I can tell 'em apart now. The dumb-waiter bell sounds like a man with a cold." Jinny talked in a low, deep voice to show what she meant. "The upstairs bell sounds like a lady screeching. That's the downstairs bell."

Carol meanwhile had pressed the button that released the downstairs door. She waited a minute or two, then opened the upstairs door. There was no one there, and she heard no footsteps coming up. Someone must have rung the wrong bell.

Then, standing in the hall, Carol had another thought. It made her feel so happy that her dimple showed for the first time since the Clarks had moved to New York. Maybe the postman had rung the bell to let them know there was a letter in their mailbox. Maybe the letter was for her, from Helen.

Carol went back into the kitchen and grabbed the little key that hung on a nail. She wanted to get the letter before the twins did.

"I hope it's for me. I hope it's for me," she kept saying to herself.

A few steps below the fourth-floor landing there was a girl on her knees, scrubbing. She got up when Carol came out. Carol saw that the girl was tall and that she had golden hair worn in two braids around her head. She wore a short gingham dress that was faded but very clean. Everything about the tall blond girl was very clean.

"Be careful when you go down the steps. I just scrubbed," the girl said.

Carol, annoyed at not being able to rush down the way she wanted to, walked carefully around the pail of water and the scrubbing brush.

"You Carol?" the girl asked. She did not seem really interested. "The twins told me to visit you, but I was too busy."

"That's all right," Carol answered. It did not seem a very polite thing to say, but it was all that she could think of. It was really all that she wanted to say. She realized that this must be Christine Swensen, the janitor's daughter.

Because the stairs were wet, Carol had to walk down slowly. She kept thinking of the letter and telling herself what she wanted it to say. She wanted the letter to say that Helen missed Carol terribly and so did all her other friends. She hoped it might even say that Bill missed her too. She wanted Helen to tell her that no one would ever take her place, just as Carol would never let anyone, not even Betsy, take Helen's place. She felt very happy as she thought of the letter that might be waiting for her downstairs.

Through the holes in the letter box marked *Clark* she saw a light-blue envelope. Carol was almost afraid to open the door of the box. The blue envelope might be a business letter for Daddy. It might be a newsy letter from one of Mother's many friends back home. It might, although Carol doubted it, even be a note for Jinny or Johnny. Carol put the key in the letter box, turned it, and took out not one letter but two.

The light-blue envelope was on top, and it was addressed in darker blue ink to *Miss Carol Clark*. Standing there in the small, hot hall, Carol smiled to herself. The letter was from Helen. She would have known that even if Helen's name and address were not written in the upper left-hand corner. Helen's teachers never liked her handwriting, but her friends admired it very much. The dots over the *i's* in *Miss* and in *City* were not just dots; they were little circles. The *t* in *City* was crossed with a long line that slanted upward.

For a minute, Carol forgot all about the other envelope. She would have read Helen's letter then and there if she had not heard a loud voice from upstairs shouting, "Hi, Chris! Need any help?" Then she heard steps rushing down. Soon Pat leaped down the last four steps. He stretched his neck to see the writing on Carol's envelope. "Letter from your boy friend?" he asked.

Carol put the envelopes behind her back. Her first thought was to say, "No, from a girl." Then she decided not to say anything. If Pat thought the letter was from a boy, let him think so. Not that it mattered what Pat thought.

"See you in the park, Carrie," Pat told her and rushed outdoors. Now Carol looked at the second letter. To her surprise, it was addressed to *Miss Henrietta M. Tyler.* Carol stared at it, trying to figure out why it had been in the Clarks' letter box. The postman must have made a mistake. Carol's first thought was to put it where it belonged, in Miss Tyler's box, which was right next to the Clarks'. Or should she give it to Miss Tyler on her way upstairs? Somehow she had the impression that Miss Tyler was a small, old, white-haired lady who carried a cane. It seemed too bad to make her walk down three flights to get the letter and then back up three flights, when Carol was going to pass her door.

Carol ran up two flights of stairs and rang the bell of the door on the third floor, just below her own. She heard footsteps coming toward the door, and she began to feel a little frightened. A hoarse voice asked who was there.

"Carol Clark. I live upstairs," Carol told her.

"What do you want?" the voice asked.

Carol tried to explain. Standing behind a closed door and talking to someone on the other side made her feel very uncomfortable. She heard the clanking of a chain, and then the door opened. The hall was so dark that for a moment Carol could not tell what Miss Tyler looked like.

Miss Tyler took the letter that Carol held out. "Come in," she said, "I want to talk to you."

Carol followed Miss Tyler into the living room. The windows were closed and the shades were down. Now Carol had a better idea of how her neighbor looked. She was very tall and very thin. She had a long thin nose, thin lips, and long thin hands. It was her hair, though, that Carol kept looking at. Miss Tyler's hair was not gray at all. It was an odd shade of orange-red. Carol wondered if it was dyed.

"You people make entirely too much noise," Miss Tyler said. Carol said she was sorry, and that Mother was trying to keep the twins quiet. "I can't stand noise," Miss Tyler interrupted. "I keep my windows closed even in summer, so I won't get all the street noises. I thought when the Dalys moved I might be blessed with quiet people upstairs. But no, I have to have three children right over my head."

The thought of being put in the same class as the twins made Carol furious. Pat had been right when he had called their neighbor Mrs. Pain-in-the-neck. Why, she even kept a broom in one corner of the living room and a chair to stand on, so she could easily knock on the ceiling when she wanted to.

Carol turned to go. As she was leaving, Miss Tyler added a few more words in the same deep, hoarse voice. "On rainy days I must have it especially quiet. I'm in the house all day because of my sinus, and I must have quiet."

Carol tried not to slam the door as she went out. She heard Mrs. Pain-in-the-neck putting the chain back on the door. She hoped the twins would jump so hard that a bulb in Mrs. Pain-in-the-neck's chandelier would fall down right on her head. In order to forget how angry she was, Carol looked down at the letter she was carrying. *Miss Carol Clark.* She was the first member of her family to receive mail at the new address.

"You took a long time getting that letter," Johnny said. Carol found herself explaining why she had been out of the apartment so long. Mother shook her head sadly. "Poor thing, she must be very unhappy," she said. The twins said Mrs. Pain-in-the-neck was going to be even more unhappy, especially on rainy days.

"Well, now I'll read my letter," Carol said and she went into the living room.

Helen had written:

Dear Carol,

I know how lonesome you must be in New York, so I thought I would write to you. I passed your house today and I wanted to cry when I thought that you would never live there any more.

Carol felt both happy and sad as she read and reread those lines. She looked up and blinked back her tears. This was exactly what she had hoped Helen would say. She continued reading:

The people who bought your house are going to move in the first of the month. They're cousins of Margie Gates, you know, and Margie told me there's a boy in the family who's ever so handsome and he's a freshman in high school, like Bill. I told Bill it's up to him to invite Margie's cousin to our house as soon as school starts.

Carol, this morning I passed the new shoe store that took all your Daddy's business away. I had promised myself that I'd never, never buy there because they are the reason you moved. But they have such nice shoes, and they're even cheaper than your Daddy's used to be. Mother said that's because they're a chain store now. I saw the cutest pair of shoes in the window, and I'm going to see if I can get Mommy to buy them for me. They'll go so well with the red dress she's making for me. You know how nice I look in red.

Have you gotten any new dresses yet? I guess you haven't had time, but I hear New York is full of stores that have the nicest things. Tell me all about your new clothes when you get them.

Well, school will be starting soon, and now that you aren't here Margie and I are going to study together like we two used to.

Please come and visit us soon and write to me often.

Love from your best friend,

Helen.

Slowly Carol put the letter back into its envelope. The joy she had felt when she read the first few lines kept fading and fading. A feeling of loneliness and disappointment took its place. Carol decided that she was being unfair to Helen. She was still so angry at Mrs. Pain-in-the-neck, she told herself, that she hadn't really paid attention to Helen's letter. She took it out of the envelope and reread it.

"Did Helen have any news?" Mother called from the kitchen.

"Nothing special," Carol answered. She always let Mother read her letters, but somehow she didn't care to show Mother this one. She told herself that she was being very silly. It was thoughtful of Helen to write so soon. It was not Helen's fault if Carol had made up a letter in her own mind and Helen had not written it. Still, Helen didn't have to sound so happy because there would be a boy living where the Clarks had lived. She didn't have to tell what nice shoes the new shoe store sold, or how she and Margie would study together when the new term began. It was plain to see that Helen was not at all lonesome.

"You must invite Helen for a weekend as soon as we get settled," Mother said from the kitchen.

"Never to this house," Carol told herself. Still feeling hurt and disappointed at Helen's letter, she walked to the window and looked out.

A big yellow truck pulled up in front of the grocery store. A man jumped out. He took one of the well-filled garbage cans from the sidewalk in front of the house and dumped its contents into a hole in the rear of the truck.

Suddenly the air was filled with the most horrible sounds. First there was a whirring sound and a rumble; then a shrill clatter, clamor, banging, and clanging, all together. The grinding seemed to go round and round, and then right through Carol. Just when it was beginning to fade, the man dumped the contents of another can into the back, and again the racket started — first the whirring and rumbling, then the clatter, clamor, banging, and clanging. Carol put her fingers in her ears. Imagine Mother expecting her to invite Helen here!

It was several minutes before the truck had

moved far enough away so that its racket was no longer deafening. The quiet, though, did not last long. Soon Carol heard Johnny and Eddie Daly, Pat's younger brother, having one of their dumb-waiter conversations. They enjoyed talking to each other through the dumb-waiter shaft more than in a room together. They told each other that it was time to go to the park.

Jinny came into the living room. "Coming to the park?" she asked. Carol said she would rather go to the library. It was cooler there, and anyway she wanted to make out a card so that she could take out books.

"Okay, Miss Stuck-up," Jinny replied. "But remember, when we all go to the Central Park Zoo or Coney Island, we won't ask you to come along."

"I won't want to go, I can assure you," Carol said in her most grown-up voice.

After a few minutes, Mother said she was going out to do her marketing. Did Carol want to go with her? Again Carol said that she was going to the library.

With Mother and the twins gone, the apartment seemed very lonely. Carol had the same feeling that she had had many years ago when she was lost. She had been only a few blocks away from home, yet everything had seemed strange and different. Now this tiny room seemed unfamiliar. The noises outside seemed unfamiliar. The furniture looked out of place. Carol wanted to cry. It was plain from Helen's letter that her old friends were beginning to forget her. The country was not home any more, and New York would never be home.

Carol was so busy feeling sorry for herself that she jumped when the upstairs doorbell rang. "Who is it?" she asked, afraid to open the door. She was glad to hear a quiet voice with a foreign accent say, "It's me, Frank. I go to the park. Maybe you come too?"

Carol opened the door and was glad to see Frank. She had seen him only once before, and she had hardly noticed him then because he was so quiet. Now she was so lonely that she was glad to go with him.

On the way downstairs, Frank said he was sorry they were late. He had been busy helping in the shop. Maybe, though, if they hurried they would still be on time for the contest.

"The contest?" Carol repeated questioningly. "What kind of contest?"

Frank seemed surprised that she did not know. "It's for the most *lentelle,*" he explained.

Carol thought she had not heard right. "*Lentelle,* what's that?" she asked.

The expression on Frank's serious face changed. He looked as unhappy as could be. "I always do that," he said, angry at himself. "I say the Italian and then I cannot say the English."

Carol told him that it really did not matter. She would find out when they reached the park. Then, to change the subject, she said that she was very glad he had called for her.

Frank looked pleased. "You see," he said, talking slowly, as if he were searching for just the right words, "I too come from far away. I know someone feels lonesome in a new place. Did you come across the ocean to get here?"

Carol explained that she hadn't crossed the ocean. She had crossed the Hudson River, which separates New York State from New Jersey. What a short distance that seemed now compared with the long distance that Frank had traveled! Why, it hardly seemed like moving at all. Frank had come to a new country as well as a new city. He had to learn a new language and new customs. "You can't help admiring him," Carol thought, "even if he is a foreigner."

Chapter 4

The Contest

CHRISTINE was sitting on the front steps as they came out. She was holding a pad on her knee and drawing. "Hi," she said, hardly looking up. Carol leaned over Christine's shoulder to see what she was drawing, and the blond girl quickly closed her pad. Carol felt herself getting angry. Who did Christine, the janitor's daughter, the girl who helped collect the garbage, think she was anyway?

Frank stopped to ask Christine if she was going to the park, and Carol was glad to hear her say that she was not.

"Christine is a wonderful artist," Frank told Carol as they walked along. "The teacher always hangs her pictures on the wall."

"My teacher always used to hang mine, too," Carol told him quickly. She was sure that Christine was not as good an artist as she was. "I like to draw gardens and flowers and things like that," she continued. "I don't know what there will be to draw in New York."

They heard voices calling their names, and both of them stopped and looked around. Betsy and Ruth were rushing after them. Ruth's plump face was hot, red, and perspiring. Her hair was mussed. Betsy, in a navy-blue cotton dress with a red belt, looked cool and even prettier than Carol had remembered.

"We thought we'd never catch up with you," said Ruth, panting.

Betsy looked at Carol's dress admiringly. "That's a lovely dress you have on. I hope it won't get soiled sitting on the grass," she said.

Carol explained that she was going to sit on a bench, not on the grass. Suddenly she had an unpleasant thought. "There *are* benches in the park, aren't there?" she asked. After all, this might be just a tiny plot of ground, not a real park at all. Betsy and Ruth both giggled and Betsy said yes, there were a few benches. Frank started to smile too, but he stopped when he saw that Carol looked annoyed. For some reason they were laughing at her, and Carol could not bear to be laughed at.

The walk was longer and hotter than Carol had expected. She decided that she had been foolish not to go to the library as she had planned.

"When is your birthday?" Ruth asked as they walked along in the hot sun. Carol said she would be twelve on October second. Ruth, who was the biggest, would not be twelve till December, and Betsy, who was the smallest, had been twelve in June. Frank said he would be twelve in November.

"I looked for my birthday on the calendar to find what day it comes on," he told the girls. "It's on Thursday, the fourth Thursday in November."

"Why, that's Thanksgiving!" Betsy exclaimed. "The schools will be closed and you'll have a whole day off for your birthday."

Frank's serious face suddenly turned bright with happiness. His eyes glowed. He drew himself up tall and straight. His voice sounded sure of itself, not timid as it had before.

"And my Cousin Maria says I am not American," he said. "*My* birthday is Thanksgiving, a great American holiday. Hers is January eighteenth and that is just like all the other days. And *she* says I am not American."

Frank was so pleased that he stopped, threw his head back, and began to laugh. Ruth and Betsy laughed too. People who passed looked at them and smiled, because they seemed so happy.

Carol started to tell Frank that his birthday would not always be on Thanksgiving, because Thanksgiving did not fall on the same date every year, but his birthday did. "But your . . ." she began.

Betsy interrupted her. "I know what you're thinking," Betsy said, taking her arm and walking quickly ahead of the others, "but don't tell him. He looks so happy. I was thinking the same thing about his birthday not always coming on Thanksgiving."

Carol had been wanting to be alone with Betsy, so they could get to know each other better. Now she said to her "Do you really like living in a neighborhood like this?" She was sure that Betsy did not like it any better than she did.

Betsy looked puzzled. "I don't know what you mean," she said.

"Oh, all these shabby buildings, one next to the other, and all the awful noise and all the people." Carol swept her hand through the air to show what she meant.

To her, the tall buildings on both sides of the narrow street looked like mountains. On the front steps sat boys and girls eating ice cream, reading comic books, blowing bubbles, coloring pictures, or just talking. On the sidewalk, in spite of the heat, there were children on skates, on bicycles, and on tricycles. There were children playing hopscotch and others playing handball against the buildings. Sometimes they dashed across the street to get the ball just as a car came along. No wonder the drivers in New York honked their horns.

Betsy looked around, too. She said hello to a woman who was sitting near an open window, sewing. "That's one of Daddy's patients," she explained to Carol. Then she answered Carol's question. "I love this neighborhood," she said seriously. "Mother and Daddy lived here when they were our age, and when Daddy got to be a doctor he didn't want to practice anywhere else."

To herself Carol said, "That explains it. Betsy never lived anywhere else, so she doesn't know how awful it is here."

Betsy had started to walk more slowly, and Ruth and Frank caught up with them.

"Carol, how about joining our club?" Ruth asked. She squeezed Carol's hand affectionately.

"I wish she wouldn't," Carol thought. "It's too hot."

"We have lots of fun," Betsy said. "Sometimes we

go bathing at Coney Island, if we can get a grown-up to come along. Sometimes we go to the movies."

Ruth interrupted. "We met at Betsy's house last week. It's too bad you weren't there. Next time we meet at Christine's."

"Just my luck," Carol thought. "I came too late to go to Betsy's, but just in time for a meeting down in the basement." Aloud, she said there was still so much work to do in the house that maybe she'd better not join the club yet. She would think about it later.

Soon they were at the entrance of a park so big that Carol couldn't see the beginning or the end of it. All she could see were trees and grass that seemed to extend for miles. She remembered wondering if New York parks had any grass.

Betsy waved her hand first in one direction, then in the other. "This is Central Park," she said, as if she were introducing a person. "It starts downtown on 59th Street and it goes all the way up to 110th Street, and from here over to Fifth Avenue."

To Carol that meant nothing, but she realized that this was a very, very big park.

"There are lots of playgrounds and a lake where you can row," Frank explained, and his voice was even prouder than Betsy's.

"It has the most beautiful flower gardens," Ruth added in the same proud voice.

"And a zoo!" Betsy joined in. "The twins are asking everyone around how you get to it."

Frank interrupted Betsy. "It has a baseball diamond, too, and . . ."

He, Betsy, and Ruth looked at one another and burst out laughing. "And benches!" they all shouted together. Carol tried to laugh too, but she was annoyed at them for laughing at her and annoyed at herself for being so wrong about Central Park.

The big green park, like the streets, was filled with people. Carol and the others walked and walked in the hot sun, and then to Carol's surprise she heard their names called. Carol saw a bandstand, and all around it, sprawled comfortably on the grass, sat boys and girls, men and women. A group of boys and girls who lived on Carol's block sat together. The twins were with them.

"Hurry and sit down or you'll be late. It's starting," Johnny shouted. That reminded Carol that she still didn't know what kind of contest it was.

Betsy, Ruth, and Frank sat down on the grass. Carol hesitated. Her light-yellow dress would certainly be stained. Nearby were many benches. "I think I'll sit on a bench," she said. No one listened to her. They were too busy saying things like, "I hope he wins! He's gotta win!" The lonesome feeling that Carol had had when she read Helen's letter returned. No one was interested in her. She walked to a bench that was not as crowded as the others and sat down.

She looked at the bandstand, and on it she saw a familiar face. What in the world was Pat Daly doing there? Leave it to Pat to be where everyone could see him, Carol thought. There were other boys and girls on the bandstand, too, and there were two men and a woman.

One of the men came forward and talked through a loud-speaker. "We're ready to start now," he shouted. "Here is our first contestant."

Everyone clapped loudly, even the grownups.

A girl stepped forward and turned her face upward, looking straight at the man. He seemed to be counting. Now the lady went through the same motions. Now they both talked to the man at the loud-speaker.

"Fifty-two per square inch," the man shouted. "Fifty-two per square inch," he repeated. Again everyone applauded. Again Carol wondered what this was all about.

One after another the boys and girls stepped forward, and the man and woman counted. Each time the man at the loud-speaker announced a number. The bigger it was, the more the people clapped.

"Now I know what kind of contest it is," Carol said to herself. It's a . . ." At that very moment Frank rushed toward her. "Freckles," he shouted and rushed back to join the others. Carol wished he would stay with her. She felt lonesome and out of things sitting here on the bench with the grownups.

As if Betsy read her thoughts, she got up, left her friends, and came to sit on the bench next to Carol. This was another chance, Carol thought, to see if she and Betsy couldn't become good friends without including the others. How should she begin? Just then Carol noticed Ruth stand up, pull down her tight dress, and sit down again. That gave her an idea. Back home, she and Helen used to feel as if they were even closer friends when they talked about someone else.

"If Ruth wore longer dresses, she wouldn't have so much trouble," Carol said to Betsy, as if she were telling her a secret. "Doesn't she ever get any new clothes?"

In a second, she realized that Betsy and Helen were not alike at all. Betsy's brown eyes grew dark with anger. Betsy looked as if she wanted to shake

Carol. She spoke very low, so that the others on the bench would not hear, but her voice trembled with fury. "That's a mean thing to say," she said. "It's cruel. Ruth's father is dead and her mother works in a factory, and Ruth and her sister Stella take care of the house and get the meals. There's never enough money for Ruth to have new dresses."

"I didn't know," Carol began. She was glad when the voice from the loud-speaker boomed across the park: "The next contestant is Patrick Daly."

Pat, wearing a bright yellow shirt, came forward, waved at the people who were applauding, and grinned from ear to ear. The twins jumped up. "Come on, Pat!" they screamed. Soon all the others, except Carol, were shouting the same thing.

The judges seemed to take longer than before. They talked excitedly to each other, nodded, counted all over again, talked some more.

Even the man at the loud-speaker seemed excited. "Sixty-five freckles per square inch!" he shouted. "Friends, we repeat, Pat Daly has sixty-five freckles per square inch, a truly amazing number of freckles."

There were several other contestants after Pat, but no one could compare with him.

At the end, the announcer held up a silver loving

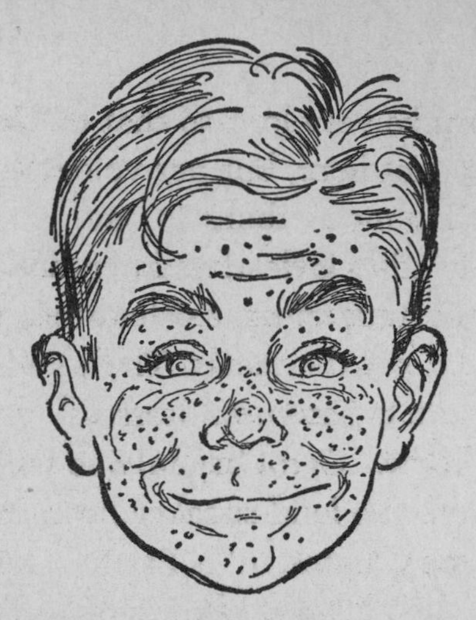

cup. “I’m just showing it to you, Pat, not giving it to you yet,” he said. “We’re going to have your name engraved on it first. And we hope, Pat, my boy, that you’ll have as many good things in your life as you have freckles on your face.”

Now the shouting, the whistling, the stamping, and the clapping were even louder than before. Carol did not join the others. She thought that never in her life had she seen people act so foolish. Why should anyone win a prize for having freckles? She had always been thankful that she didn’t have a single one. Helen had felt the same way. That reminded Carol that she must answer Helen's letter soon. So far, though, there wasn't anything Carol wanted to tell her.

Pat rushed down from the bandstand toward his friends. Betsy jumped up and hurried toward the others. Carol followed her slowly. Pat stopped every few steps to shake hands with people who congratulated him. When he reached his friends, he said, "You can touch me for luck, kids, and from now on you can call me Champ."

Johnny pushed toward Pat and put a finger over a group of Pat's freckles. "For luck," he shouted. "Everyone touch Pat for luck." Jinny followed his example, and one person after another did the same thing. Carol drew back. She felt embarrassed because her brother and sister and all the other boys and girls were acting so silly.

Suddenly a voice boomed through the loudspeaker again. "Wait a minute, everybody. Don't go yet. I've been reminded to remind you not to forget the art contest at the library. Prizes for the best original pictures. Remember there's only one week left to hand in your art work. Winners will be announced on August first. Don't forget, kids. There's a prize for children from five to nine, and one for boys and girls from ten to fourteen." When the man shouted the last words, Carol felt that he was talking directly to her.

On the way home, everyone crowded around Pat. Carol walked a little behind the others, not lonely or unhappy now, but humming to herself. Let Pat show off all he pleased today. Let him think he was a hero because he had a lot of ugly red freckles. There was an art contest on. On August first she would have her day.

"If it's an art contest, I'll win. I know I will," she told herself. Drawing had always been her favorite subject. She had won a prize in school last year for a picture of Sir Galahad and his horse. She would drop in at the library the first chance she got to see what the rules were. She would work all next week on the picture. She would show these New York people, especially Betsy, that being a real artist was more important than having freckles. And it would be wonderful to be able to write to Helen and say, "I won first prize in an art contest here." Carol decided that she would not answer Helen's letter until the contest was over and she could write her that news.

Yes, this was Pat's day, but August first would be hers.

Chapter 5

Carol Gets Busy

THAT EVENING, the twins could talk about nothing but Pat and the freckle contest. They talked about Pat during dinner and while the dishes were being washed and put away. Their eyes shone with pride every time they mentioned Pat's name. They could not seem to believe their luck. Imagine living right under the winner of a freckle contest!

Again Carol thought, as she had so often since the Clarks moved to New York, that the twins were very silly. She tried to remember how she had been when she was eight and a half. She did not remember ever seeming as young and foolish as the twins.

"There's an art contest being held at the library,"

Carol told Mother and Dad when Jinny and Johnny had both stopped talking at the same minute.

Immediately Daddy looked interested. He put down the paper he had been trying to read while the twins were chatting. "An art contest? That's just your kind of thing, Carol. Tell us about it."

Carol said that she would not know much about the contest until she inquired at the library tomorrow. She did know that there was only one week left to submit her drawings and that the prize winners would be announced two weeks after that, on the first day of August. Carol tried to sound as if she were just talking to keep up the conversation, not as if she were seriously interested.

"You get into that contest, Carol," Daddy said. "You draw very well." He turned to Mother. "Don't you think she has a good chance of winning?"

Mother said that Carol certainly did have a chance to win, and that even if she didn't win, entering a contest was always fun. Carol disagreed, but she didn't say so. She could not explain that the only reason she was going to enter the contest was to win first prize. She had to make these New York girls and boys look up to her. She had to make that show-off Pat realize that he was not so important. She had to make Betsy understand that Carol had a good reason for feeling superior. She felt herself getting angry when she remembered Betsy's voice saying, "That's a mean thing to say." Well, after August first, Betsy would not talk to her that way.

The next day Carol went to the library and found out about the contest. There were to be two prizes of ten dollars each. One was for the boy or girl under nine whose picture was considered best. The other was for the boy or girl ten and over. Then there would be two honorable mentions. These two people would each get a certificate and a letter to a bookstore, allowing them to choose any book they wanted, free. Carol had until six o'clock on Saturday to get her drawing in.

There were a few other things that Carol found out. The drawing had to be original, not a copy of another drawing. The artist had to put his or her name, address, and age on the back of the picture, not the front. The pictures would be hung on the walls of the children's room in the library for two weeks, and then a committee of artists would choose the best ones.

Carol could hardly wait to start on her drawing. She made the twins promise that they would not tell anyone she was going to submit a picture. Half the fun of winning would be to see how surprised the boys and girls would be when they heard her name announced in the library. She could imagine them crowding around her as they had crowded around Pat. "We didn't even know you were in the contest. Why didn't you tell us?" they would say. Carol would only smile and shrug her shoulders.

"We'll keep it a secret if you tell us what the picture is going to be about," Johnny promised. Carol said that she was not going to tell anyone, not even Mother and Daddy, until the picture was finished.

"I'll tell you what we'll do," said Daddy. "We'll pretend it's a real exhibition and we'll have an unveiling. Mother will make a curtain to cover the picture. When it's finished, you hang the picture on the wall, cover it, draw the curtain, and let us all look at it. How's that?"

What a wonderful idea! "Would you really make the curtain that we could pull?" Carol asked Mother, and her blue eyes glowed with excitement. She could picture the room when she showed the picture. Mother, Daddy, and even the twins would be so impressed that at first they wouldn't say a word. The room would be completely silent. Then they would clap and clap.

There was something else Carol wanted to talk about before she started to work on the picture. She didn't want any interruptions. Mother and Daddy said she could work in their room. The light was good there, and the twins would not run in and out. Carol decided not to go outdoors with the girls during the next week or to have them visit. Mother and the twins would have to take care of that somehow.

"I know! We'll tell everyone you have scarlet fever and you can't go out, and they can't visit you or they'll catch it," Jinny suggested.

"No, that's not so good," Johnny decided. "No one'll come near us either. And they'll quarantine us like they did in the country when we really had scarlet fever."

Jinny was thinking seriously. "We could say she broke her leg and she's in the hospital," she suggested.

Johnny did not like that idea. "They'll wanna visit her," he said. "Let's say she was kidnaped and we don't know where she is." He looked very pleased at his plan and seemed surprised when Mother and Daddy burst out laughing.

"Stop making up stories," Mother said. "You can just tell them Carol is busy."

The next few days were rainy and dreary. In a way Carol was glad. Mother did not urge her to go outside. The rain made the air cooler, too, so that she could work more comfortably.

In other ways the dark, dreary weather made

things harder. First, the light was not good. The twins could not go outdoors, so they invited their friends in. Through the closed door of the bedroom Carol could hear shouting, laughing, jumping, and banging on the piano. She could also hear the repeated thump-thump-thumps on the floor. She remembered Mrs. Pain-in-the-neck saying that she must have quiet on rainy days because her sinus bothered her and she had to stay home. Carol wondered if Mrs. Pain-in-the-neck did not wish that the Dalys lived above her again.

Often, after Mrs. Pain-in-the-neck had knocked with more vigor than usual, Mother sent Johnny, Jinny, and their friends upstairs to visit Eddie Daly. Then, as Carol drew, she heard shouts and stamping on the ceiling above her head. The twins had never seemed so noisy in the country. Maybe it was because Carol was not always so close to them. She sighed as she thought of the big, roomy house they had left.

It was that very house Carol was drawing from memory. She remembered everything about it — the flat-topped roof, the porch with the comfortable chairs and the hammock on it, the flower garden in front, the tall trees in back, and the blue sky above. Carol loved drawing it and painting in all the famil-

iar colors. She wondered if the librarian would return her picture so that she could show it to Helen. On August second she would surely answer Helen's letter. She would be too excited on August first, and there would be too many people to talk with.

Saturday morning, when Carol looked at the completed water color, she felt sad and glad at the same time. She was glad because it was so good. The house, however, looked so real that Carol almost cried with loneliness. She tried not to look out the window. She did not want to see the tall, dirty gray buildings with their ugly fire escapes.

Carol took her picture into the living room and covered it with the red curtain Mother had made. It had a cord pulled through the hem at the top. Carol's heart was beating quickly as she tacked up the curtain. What would the others think of her picture?

At noon, the twins rushed in with Daddy. "It's up! It's up!" Johnny yelled. He was as excited as Carol herself and she felt like hugging him for being so enthusiastic. How proud the twins would be on August first when she won a ten-dollar prize! They would tell everyone in the neighborhood, and people Carol didn't even know would come up to congratulate her.

"Do you want to see the picture before lunch or after lunch?" Mother asked.

"Before lunch," three voices shouted together, and Daddy's was almost as loud as the twins'.

The four Clarks sat close together on the sofa, facing the picture. Carol stood on one side of it. She waited. Everyone was very still. Even the outside noises seemed quieter than usual. Carol's fingers trembled as she drew the cord.

"It's our old house!" Johnny screamed at the top of his voice.

"It's where we used to live!" Jinny shouted. There was no question in Carol's mind that the twins liked her picture very much.

Carol looked at her mother. The room was very still. Carol saw that there were tears in Mother's eyes. Daddy looked at Mother in a startled and worried way.

"I'm just a plain fool," Mother said, wiping her eyes. "I don't know why I did that. The picture is lovely, Carol, perfectly lovely." Mother came over and kissed her.

Daddy put his arm across her shoulder and hugged her. "I'm very proud of you," he said.

The twins talked during lunch, but the other three were quiet. Carol kept thinking about Mother. The tears in her eyes had told Carol many things that Mother had hidden since they moved to New York. She missed the country and the big house as much as Carol did, maybe even more. She did not like this tiny, crowded apartment on a noisy street any more than Carol did. It had been just as hard for her to give up her old friends and make new ones. But she had not complained, because she did not want to hurt Daddy. For the first time Carol forgot her own unhappiness about their new home.

Mother helped Carol wrap the picture carefully. "Good luck, darling," she said when Carol started for the library.

Outside the house Carol met Ruth and Christine. "Where are you going?" Ruth asked. Carol said just for a walk. She did not want the girls to know that she was going to the library to leave the picture.

"We'll walk with you," Ruth said. Christine said nothing, but walked along beside Ruth.

Carol wondered how she could get rid of them. "I'm going for a long walk, and it's hot," she said. "Maybe you'd better not come."

Ruth said she didn't mind the heat at all.

Christine stopped short. "Come on back, Ruthie. Don't you know when you're not wanted?" she said, giving Ruth's arm a little pull. Ruth stood there and looked at Carol questioningly.

Carol knew Ruth wanted her to urge them to come with her. But she couldn't, for she had to be alone.

"So long," she said to Ruth and Christine. Ruth blinked back tears. She looked hurt.

"On August first I'll explain everything. She'll understand then," Carol told herself.

The librarian thanked Carol for the picture and told her it would be Number 44, and that Carol could see it on the wall of the children's room on Tuesday. No, she said in answer to Carol's question, there were not as many pictures handed in as they had hoped. Evidently boys and girls did not feel like working during the summer. That, thought Carol, made her chances of winning even better.

Carol felt happy as she left the library. In fact, she felt so pleased with herself that when Pat visited the Clarks that evening she was friendlier to him than usual. Pat came in carrying an old black shoe. The twins were as excited over his visit as if he were President of the United States. They brought him a chair and sat where they could look at him. Daddy kept staring at the worn old shoe in Pat's hand.

"Know why I came?" Pat asked. Before anyone could answer, he explained. "I've been helping at the garage Saturdays and Sundays and time off. I don't get paid, just tips. Well, I saved five bucks and I want to get Mom a pair of shoes. She wants me to get pants, but she sure needs the new shoes even more than I need pants, so I'm gonna get her a pair for her birthday."

A look of understanding crossed Daddy's face.

"Mom's got her bedroom slippers on now, so I sneaked off with her shoe," Pat continued. "I hope she doesn't look for it. She bought it at your place, Mr. Clark, and I wanna get her another pair just like it, if it doesn't come to more than five dollars."

Daddy took the old shoe and looked inside. He wrote down the style and size. "It's four dollars, Pat, so you'll have a dollar left for yourself," Daddy said.

Pat's grin spread from ear to ear. "Gee, that's great. I'll get Mom a pair of nylons. She'll pretend to be sore, all right."

Carol kept feeling friendlier and friendlier toward Pat. He had not called her Carrie once this evening. He was not chewing bubble gum and he had not shouted or shown off about anything. And it was very nice of him to buy shoes for his mother when he really did need trousers himself.

She felt a little sorry for Pat. On August first it would be Carol, not Pat, who would be getting all the attention. She wondered how he would like that. It was all these things together that made her say, "We were just going to have lemonade. Want some?"

"You bet I do," Pat told her. He followed her into the kitchen and watched while she took a pitcher of cold lemonade out of the icebox. She poured the golden liquid into tall glasses.

"You know, Carrie," Pat said, "you're not as bad as some of the kids think."

Carol was so startled that she spilled some of the lemonade on the table. While she mopped it up, she kept her face turned so that Pat would not see how red it was. She hardly touched her drink when they were back in the living room. Pat finished it for her.

In bed that night, Carol kept thinking of what Pat had said. "You're not as bad as some of the kids think." Had he been teasing? Carol did not think so. The girls had been talking about her, that was plain. Well, who cared what they thought? On August first they would be making a fuss over her, all right. She wasn't hurt. She didn't care.

Jinny pushed her. "Hey, what are you sniffing about?" she asked.

Chapter 6

A Visit to the Library

CAROL could hardly wait for Tuesday to come. Tuesday was the day when all the pictures would be hung on the library walls. She planned to wake up very early on Tuesday morning and be the first one in the library. Maybe the librarian would not be so busy then and would look at the name on Carol's card. Then she would smile and say, "So you're the Carol Clark who submitted that lovely picture. It's by far the best one that was handed in." As Carol repeated that sentence to herself, she felt happy all over. It would not be so bad to live in New York if everyone around here looked up to her.

When Tuesday morning came, Carol's pillow was damp with perspiration. The small bedroom, even with the window wide open, was as hot as a furnace. Quietly, so that she would not wake Jinny, Carol got out of bed. She looked out of the window at the clotheslines. Not even a handkerchief was moving. There was no breeze whatever. Even the thought of seeing how her painting looked on the library wall could not make Carol hurry on such a hot day.

At breakfast, Daddy turned on the radio to hear the news. "This will probably be the hottest day on record," a man's voice said. Daddy mopped his forehead. "It's expected to reach ninety-eight degrees by noon and go even higher in the early afternoon," the announcer continued. Daddy, who had finished his breakfast, started to get up but he stuck to the chair, which came up with him. The twins, who had just come into the kitchen, were delighted. They sat down, tried to get up, and brought their chairs up with them too.

"Promise me none of you will go out till later in the day," Daddy said to all the family. Then he turned to Mother. "Don't even go to the grocery store. Open some cans."

"But this is the first day I can see my picture in the library," Carol protested. Daddy said that the picture would not walk off the wall.

The city grew steadily hotter — and quieter, as people rested in their apartments, away from the blazing streets. Then, about four o'clock, the curtains began to stir a little.

"There's a breeze! Look at the curtain!" Jinny shouted.

"Let's go out," Johnny yelled.

Carol decided to go out with them and walk to the library. The twins ran down the four flights of stairs ahead of her and rushed across the street to call for some friends. Carol stood in front of the building for a moment. She looked up and down the street, but saw no one she knew. The block seemed strangely quiet. The quiet lasted for only a minute. Then she heard the shouts of Jinny, Johnny, and two of their friends.

"It's easy for the twins to make friends," Carol thought, and for the first time she felt a little jealous of them. When school began, they would feel at home in their new class, because they already knew so many children. At the thought of entering a new class in a new school, Carol felt lonelier than she had at any time since the move to New York.

"It's the heat that's making me feel so kind of sad," she told herself. "I'll get someone to go to the library with me, and then I won't feel like this. Ruth would be just the right person. Asking her to go to the library now would be like apologizing for not asking her that other time." Carol really felt sorry she had hurt Ruth's feelings. She had not meant to. Well, on August first Ruth would understand.

Carol walked to Ruth's house and rang the bell, but no one was at home. She decided to try Maria. First she would go into the shoe-repair shop and see if Maria was there.

The shop was cool and peaceful, and alive with quiet, pleasant sounds. Carol heard a machine whirring rhythmically as Frank's father, his back turned to her, worked on a woman's shoe. She heard the tap, tap, tap of the hammer that Frank's uncle was using to put a new heel on a pump. She heard the swish of Frank's cloth as he put the last shine on a man's brown shoes. The man got down from the shoeshine chair, paid Frank, and left the store.

For the first time Frank saw Carol standing near the door. His dark eyes brightened. "Well, *he* likes me anyway," Carol thought. She guessed it was because she, like Frank, had moved to New York from a place that was quite different. Whatever the reason, Carol felt a pleasant glow at the thought that Frank liked her. She asked him if Maria was at home.

Frank seemed embarrassed as he answered. He did not look directly at Carol when he said that Maria was not at home. Carol said she was sorry, for she was going to the library and wanted company.

Frank's uncle said something in Italian. "My uncle says I have been in the store long enough and I should go out," Frank explained. "I will go to the library with you."

The children's room at the library looked altogether different now that the pictures were hung. Carol's eyes went straight to her painting. It looked pretty, she thought, much prettier than the pictures on all sides of it. She decided not to point it out to Frank, but to see what he would say when they reached it.

They began with the picture nearest to the door. Carol wished that she could rush Frank past the silly pictures of people, cats, dogs, horses, and bowls of flowers, straight to her own picture. Frank, however, stopped and studied each picture carefully. If only he would hurry!

"This one is beautiful," Frank exclaimed enthusiastically, as he and Carol stopped in front of the next picture.

"Beautiful?" Carol repeated in surprise. "It's drawn well, but I'd never call it beautiful."

It was the picture of a row of tall gray buildings, all exactly the same, with fire escapes running up and down each one. On the sidewalk in front of the buildings were garbage cans. Near one can the artist had drawn a kitten playing with a piece of orange peel. It might have been any block in the neighborhood.

To Carol, the picture was ugly, just as her own street was ugly. "Whoever drew it draws well, but I don't like the picture," she said again to Frank. He kept looking at it as if he did not want to move. Carol felt like pushing him toward her picture. They would never get to it if Frank did not hurry a little.

Now they were directly in front of Carol's picture. Her heart pounded as she looked up at Frank. His eyes were bright and he was smiling. "This is very pretty, too," he said. "In Italy rich people live in such houses. Here I have not seen them."

"But there are lots of them," Carol told him. Her voice was more excited than she had expected it to be. "You haven't seen any part of the United States except New York."

Frank agreed. "And I have not seen any part of New York except the part where we live," he admitted. "You are right. I cannot judge this picture as well as the other one." His eyes went back to the picture of the apartment houses.

On their way home Carol, trying not to sound especially interested, asked Frank which picture he thought would win the prize. She never learned the answer, for just then they were in front of the subway station and a crowd of people rushed up the stairs. Carol heard familiar voices and lots of cheerful laughter.

"There are the girls," Frank said.

Carol saw Betsy, Maria, Christine, Ruth, and an older girl who looked very much like Ruth. They were so busy talking as they climbed the stairs that they did not notice Carol and Frank waiting at the top.

The girls looked happy, and somehow different. Carol realized it was their deep sunburn that made the difference. Christine's burn made her green eyes look larger and greener, and her blond hair even more golden. Betsy's light skin looked red and sore. Maria, Ruth, and Ruth's sister looked tanned and healthy.

Carol had the same feeling of envy that she had had when the twins rushed across the street to join their friends. The girls must have been having a wonderful time.

Frank was so embarrassed at the meeting that Carol realized he had known all along where Maria and the others were. He had known that they had not invited her to go with them. Well, she would show them all that she didn't care.

"Have a good time?" she asked.

"Swell!" Christine answered in a cold voice. "We went swimming at Coney Island. It was wonderful." Her voice showed that she was trying to make Carol envious.

Frank said he wanted to get back to the store and he hurried ahead.

"The water was cold," Betsy said, pretending to shiver.

"The waves kept knocking us over every time we went in," Maria continued.

Carol felt that they were all trying to make her envious — all but Ruth. Ruth frowned and looked worried. Carol decided not to show them that she cared. She would talk about something else.

"I went to your house to call for you," she said to Ruth. "You weren't home, so I called for Maria and she wasn't home, so Frank and I went to the library together to see the pictures."

She was surprised when the girls stopped and looked at one another. Again Ruth looked as if she were about to cry. "We should have," she said to Christine. Christine shrugged her shoulders. Carol could not figure out what the girls meant.

By now they were in front of Betsy's house. "So long," Betsy said. "I hope my face won't be all blisters by tomorrow."

Ruth and her sister reached their home next, and Maria went upstairs with them to borrow a book.

Christine and Carol walked along, and neither one spoke for a minute or two. Then Christine turned to Carol. "Don't blame Ruthie or Maria for not inviting you," she said sharply. "They both wanted to, but I said it was you or me. Betsy didn't care one way or the other. If you were too stuck-up to come to the meeting at my house, then I didn't want to go to Coney Island with you." Christine held her blond head very high.

"I didn't know when the meeting was," Carol replied.

Christine said that she had gone upstairs to invite Carol and had left the message with the twins.

"The twins didn't tell me," Carol said. It was true that the twins had forgotten to tell her, but she would not have gone anyway. She had decided that day in the park not to go. Anyway, the meeting had taken place during the week when Carol had been working on her picture. Still, she was glad now that she could say the twins had not told her.

Christine stared hard at Carol. "Maybe I've got you wrong," she said. "Maybe you're not really a snob like I thought you were. Say, do you want to go to Coney Island with us next time?"

Carol said she would be very glad to go.

Christine went down the steps to her basement apartment and Carol started to climb the three flights to her home. She was thinking of how happy the girls had looked. She remembered how gay their laughter had sounded as they climbed the subway stairs. Again she thought that they must have had a wonderful time.

Carol hoped that they would invite her when they went to Coney Island again. She had never been there, but she had heard about the big beach and the boardwalk where you could buy all kinds of souvenirs, as well as all kinds of things to eat. And what fun it must be to bathe in the ocean and be knocked over by waves!

Going to Coney Island with the girls would really be something to write to Helen about. "I went to Coney Island today with four of my new friends and the older sister of one of them. You should see how sunburned I am. I hope my face won't be all blisters tomorrow." That would make Helen realize that Carol was getting along without her, just as she seemed to be getting along without Carol. The only trouble was that it had not happened. Somehow she was not really getting along at all.

Chapter 7

The Prize

THE TWO WEEKS between the day when Carol handed in her picture and the date for giving out the prizes seemed more like two years. Every day during those two weeks, except Sunday when the building was closed, Carol visited the library. Every time she looked around at the decorated walls. "Forget which picture is yours, and see which you'd give the prize to if you were the judge," she told herself over and over again. There was no doubt in her mind at all.

Carol often looked at "City Street," the picture Frank had admired so much. Yes, it was well drawn, but she didn't like to look at such an unpleasant scene. It was bad enough to look out of the window and see a row of gray buildings with fire escapes and garbage cans. Who in the world would want to look at it in a picture?

At last the day really came — the day for the awards. Carol hoped that the girls would call for her and they would all walk to the library together and sit in a group. When her name was announced as prize winner, Carol wanted to see the admiration and surprise in the faces around her.

It was Maria who called for Carol. She seemed much excited. "The others are waiting for me in the store," she said. "We're all going together, and I thought you'd want to come with us too." Carol noticed that Maria had said, "The others are waiting for *me*" — not "for *us*." Maria's dark eyes looked even darker than usual. "Won't it be wonderful if someone we know wins?" she said.

All at once Carol had a thought. Was it possible that Maria had submitted a picture too? Was that why she was so excited? Then Carol had another thought. Was it possible that "City Street" was hers?

Ruth, Betsy, and Christine were waiting in the shoe-repair shop downstairs. As they walked toward the library, Carol kept hoping they would find seats in the first row so she would not have to push her way to the front to get the prize. However, they found the room already half filled with laughing, chattering boys and girls. All the front seats were taken. Jinny and Johnny sat in the very first row with their friends.

"Hey, Carol, know which picture I like best?" Johnny called as Carol walked toward him. Carol held her breath for a second. Those brats! Leave it to them to tell everyone which was her picture.

Jinny winked at Johnny. "We like the picture of the cat," she said, pointing in the direction of a fluffy white cat. "Our friend Tim drew it. It's his cat."

Carol breathed a sigh of relief.

In a few minutes the librarian, Miss Horn, knocked on the table for quiet. The buzz became fainter, then disappeared entirely. Miss Horn introduced Mr. Bond, a famous artist. Everyone clapped as he came forward, and the girls stretched their necks to see him. Mr. Bond told how much he liked children's drawings. He said that this was a very good exhibition. He told jokes, and everyone laughed but Carol. She wished that he would stop wasting time and announce the winners. How could Christine, sitting next to her, look so amused at Mr. Bond's stories?

At last he began to talk about the winners. "I know the younger winners are the most impatient," Mr. Bond said, "so I'll break the news to them first. The first prize for children nine and under goes to Tim Henderson for the picture called 'My Cat.' Come on up, Tim."

Everyone applauded and stamped and sat forward to see who Tim was. No one rose and no one came to the front of the room.

Suddenly Johnny's loud voice rang out. "Get up, Tim, or I'll push you."

The boys and girls giggled, and a small boy wearing glasses got up and went toward Mr. Bond. His face was very red. Carol hoped that she would not be as frightened when her turn came.

There was more applause when a girl won the honorable mention and received a letter with which she could get any book she wanted. She was not shy like Timmy. She pushed her way to the front and bowed to the others.

"It's a good thing she's so young," Carol thought. "She seems to think that second best is good. I'd rather not get anything than get second best."

When the wave of applause died down, Mr. Bond took his place again. Carol's heart beat rapidly. She found herself breathing fast.

Again Mr. Bond chatted as if he had all the time

in the world. "The older contestants made things hard for us," he said, after telling a few stories and jokes. "They were too good. We wished we had ten prizes to give out instead of only two. After a lot of thinking, we decided who should get first prize and who should get honorable mention. Then we noticed something unusual. The two winners were both girls. What happened to you boys? What's more, the two girls live at the same address." Mr. Bond paused.

The boys and girls began to talk about what a strange thing that was — two winners at the same address.

Now Carol's heart beat even faster. She had been right about Maria. Maria had entered the contest and won honorable mention. That was why Frank liked "City Street" so much, and that was why Maria had seemed so excited when she called for Carol.

Mr. Bond held up his hand for quiet. "We judges could hardly believe that the winner of the first prize was a girl only twelve years old. The picture is so well drawn that it might have been done by a much older artist. We predict a great future for Christine Swensen, who drew 'City Street.' "

Carol heard two loud gasps. One was her own. One came from Christine, whose face had turned white and who sat up with a start.

"It's a mistake," Carol told herself. "Sit quietly and he'll correct himself. It's a mistake."

The clapping, stamping, and whistling around her did not seem real. The happiness that shone in the faces of Ruth, Betsy, and Maria seemed just as unreal. The only thing that seemed real to Carol was the dream she had had for the last two weeks. This was to be *her* special day, not Christine's. It was not fair!

Ruth touched Carol and pointed to her hands. Carol realized that she was the only one who was not clapping. She joined the others and forced herself to smile.

Mr. Bond silenced them again by raising his hand. "Now for the honorable mention and the certificate for a book. That award goes to a delightful picture, a very pleasing water color called 'Country Home.' It is by Carol Clark of the same address as Christine's. That's really quite a place for artists."

This did not seem real either to Carol. She had to tell herself that the applause and the stamping were for her. She heard the shrill voices of the twins yelling, "Yippee! Carol won! Hurray for Carol!" She felt Ruth pushing her, then whispering, "Go up for the certificate." Still she did not seem able to move. "Second prize," she told herself. "Who wants to win second prize?"

Then another voice filled the room, and it made her really sit up. "Hey, Carrie, get up and take a bow," shouted Pat through his cupped hands. Soon other boys and girls were screaming, "Hey, Carrie, get up and take a bow."

Carol felt herself growing flaming red. It was bad enough to win second prize, but to be called Carrie in front of all these people and to have everyone looking at her and shouting at her — that was too much. She hated Pat Daly and she always would.

Carol got up, walked stiffly to the front of the room, and tried to look pleased as Mr. Bond congratulated her. She took the certificate and went back to her seat. She wished that she could vanish into the air. She wished that she could run home, throw herself on the bed, and cry. It was not to win second prize that she had entered the contest. Now everyone would think of her as all right, but nowhere near as good an artist as Christine.

When they all rose to leave the library, a crowd of people gathered around Christine and Carol.

"I'm so proud of you both," Ruth said. "Imagine having two friends who are wonderful artists!"

Christine, usually so cool, squeezed Ruth's hand. "Gosh, I'm happy!" she said. She turned to Carol. "Aren't you?"

"Not especially," Carol answered truthfully. "He said he predicted a great future for you, not for me." The minute she said it Carol wished that she had not. She should not have shown the girls how unhappy she was. She should be pretending to be pleased. Somehow, even though she knew she was saying the wrong things, Carol could not seem to stop talking. "He just said mine was 'delightful and pleasing.'" She could see the girls looking at one another as if they did not know what to say. She saw Christine shrug her shoulders.

The walk home was not so different from the way Carol had imagined it. She was surrounded by people who said flattering, pleasant things. But the things they said were meant *first* for Christine, *then* for her. She tried to smile politely, but her lips were stiff. If only her picture had not been chosen at all! Then no one would know that she had handed one in, and no one would be seeing how jealous and unhappy she was. It would have been much better not to have won anything than to have won second prize. And Pat yelling at her that way and calling her Carrie! Carol bit her lips at the thought. The day she had looked forward to was one of the unhappiest of her life.

"Let's all go up to my house for a while," Betsy suggested. "There's lemonade in the refrigerator and we have cookies, and we'll have a party to celebrate our two winners."

Christine said she would run ahead and tell her father the good news; then she would come right back. Maria and Ruth accepted Betsy's invitation immediately. Betsy looked at Carol. Carol hesitated. She liked to visit Betsy, even though she realized now that Betsy would never be her best friend. At this moment, however, the only thing she wanted was to be alone. She had been polite and smiling as long as she could.

"Maybe I'll come after I tell my mother about the . . ." Carol gulped. The next two words came out with difficulty. "The honorable mention. Don't wait for me, though. I might not come."

Betsy's smile vanished. "We won't wait," she said a little angrily. "Do just as you please."

Carol hoped that the twins would be out when she reached home, but evidently they were not. When she came to the third floor, a door opened a few inches. "Wait, I want to talk to you," said a deep voice.

Carol stopped and stood just outside the door, while Miss Tyler stood inside. Carol knew what her neighbor was going to say. As she stood at the doorway she heard a loud crash from the floor above.

"Do you hear that?" Miss Tyler asked.

3B

Now Carol could hear loud piano playing. Thud, thud, thud! One of the twins was pressing the pedal to the floor. Miss Tyler stood there and said nothing for a few moments.

"I want you to tell your mother to see that the noise stops — not only the piano banging but the dumb-waiter conversations that your sister and brother have with anyone who'll listen to them. By now everyone in the building knows that you and the Swensen girl have won prizes. Your brother and sister went down to the basement and rang each dumb-waiter bell in the building to tell the news. Personally, I do not care. All I care about is quiet."

Carol mumbled that she would see what she could do. Her anger at Mrs. Pain-in-the-neck almost made her forget her disappointment about the prize. "She's a mean old woman," Carol thought angrily. "I'll never do a thing to help her. Even if she fell down and broke her leg, I wouldn't. I'd leave her on the floor."

There was no chance to rush into her room without being seen. Mother opened the door for her. "I'm so happy about the prize," she exclaimed. "I asked Maria's mother if I could use her phone, and I called your father at the store. That's how excited I was. He's so proud of you, Carol."

"Proud of what?" Carol asked.

Her voice was so sharp that Mother looked at her in surprise. "Proud of his daughter's winning second prize, of course. Imagine being the second-best artist in this whole big neighborhood!"

"Second to Christine," Carol said, as she went into her bedroom. She began to comb her hair in front of the mirror.

Mother followed her into the bedroom and sat on the chair. "I'm very proud of you, Carol," she said. "What I mean is that I'm proud you have a talent *for art.*" She said the last two words — *for art* — very slowly, and she emphasized them. Her voice sounded serious.

"Why did you say *for art* that way?" Carol asked, facing her mother.

Mother sighed. "You won't like what I'm going to say, Carol," she told her. "I mean you have a talent for art and some for music too, but you have no talent for friendship, and in lots of ways that's more important. Your father and I are worried about the way you act toward the children in the neighborhood. They've all been very nice to you, but now they're not as friendly as they were. I don't blame them a bit. You can't expect them to be friendly when you act so cold and superior."

Carol hated being lectured, and because she was so disappointed anyway she felt the tears coming to her eyes. She was glad when the twins began banging at the piano. That gave her a chance to talk about something else.

"Mrs. Pain-in-the-neck stopped me on the way upstairs and told me you have to stop making so much noise," Carol called from the bedroom into the living room.

In less than a minute the twins were in the bedroom with her. "Tell us what she said. Hurry up and tell us," Jinny demanded.

Carol told them. She was so glad to be able to talk about Miss Tyler instead of the prizes or her unfriendliness that she told the twins and Mother everything Miss Tyler had said. She even told them what she had said to herself on the way from the third floor to the fourth. The twins threw back their dark, curly heads and shouted with laughter.

"If she breaks a leg, we'll leave her on the floor," Johnny repeated again and again. He began jumping up and down as he said it. Jinny joined him and made up a little rhyme. "We won't do one thing more — we'll leave her on the floor. We won't do one thing more — we'll leave her on the floor." She and Johnny both recited it over and over.

"You awful children," said Mother, but she laughed. Carol, glad to laugh at anything, joined them. Mother stopped laughing and said, "Don't forget that silly poem if you ever do see anyone with a broken leg. Don't try to move them or anything. Just leave them alone and call a doctor."

"We won't do one thing more — we'll leave her on the floor," shouted the twins.

Thump! Thump! Thump! Mother and Carol exchanged startled looks. Carol said, "You don't think she heard, do you?"

"Of course not," Mother replied. "But that's what I thought too. It shows our conscience bothers us for being so unkind. What an unhappy, friendless woman Miss Tyler must be!"

All at once Carol no longer wanted to make fun of Miss Tyler. When Mother said "friendless," Carol felt afraid. When Miss Tyler was eleven and a half, maybe she didn't have what Mother called a "talent for friendship." Maybe if you weren't friendly when you were Carol's age, you were like Miss Tyler when you grew up. Maybe once upon a time Miss Tyler didn't think any of the girls in her neighborhood were good enough for her. Although it was a hot day, Carol shivered as if she had a chill.

Chapter 8

Where Are the Twins?

"DID YOU THINK over the thing we were talking about?" Daddy asked Mother the next Friday evening.

All the Clarks were in the kitchen. Mother, who had just finished washing the dishes in hot, sudsy water, was now scrubbing the pots and pans. Carol was drying the dishes and the twins were polishing the silver. Daddy put the dishes back on the cabinet shelves as fast as Carol dried them.

Mother looked up from the pot she was scouring, but before she could even open her mouth to answer Daddy, the twins asked a stream of questions. "Think over what? What are you talking about? What's the secret? Why don't you tell us?"

Daddy smiled. Slowly and carefully he put the dishes away, without saying anything; then he explained. The next morning he and a man he worked with were going to drive to the shoe factory. There was room in the car for one more person. Daddy paused.

The twins looked at each other, looked at Carol, and looked at Mother. Who would the one person be?

"Who do you think should go?" Daddy asked.

Three voices shouted, "Mother!"

Daddy looked at Mother, smiled, and said, "See?" Then he turned to Carol and the twins. "I thought your mother needed a nice ride and a change, too. She's been working very hard since we moved to New York. The trouble is that she doesn't like to leave you kids alone from morning till night, and we'd have to leave early."

"You used to leave us alone all day back home," Carol reminded Mother.

"That's what I told her," Daddy said. "But your mother says it's different in New York. She's afraid you'll get run over or kidnaped or something." Daddy looked at Carol in a special way, as if he were trying to tell her something.

Carol drew herself up tall and tossed her blond head. She turned to Mother. "After all, I'm almost twelve," she said. "I should think you could trust me to look after Jinny and Johnny for one day."

"Look after us!" the twins screamed indignantly. "Who needs looking after, I'd like to know?" Johnny added.

Jinny threw back her dark, curly head just as her sister had done. She drew herself up tall, too. "After all, we're almost nine," she said in her most grown-up voice.

That gave Johnny an idea. He flung his towel across the towel rack and motioned to his twin to do the same. "If we're too young to take care of ourselves, we're too young to polish the silver," he said. Then, with Jinny close behind him, he stomped out of the kitchen. The minute they were in the living room, they burst out laughing. The three in the kitchen laughed too.

When Mother stopped laughing, she said that she did not want to insult her children, so she would go with Daddy. "I'll leave plenty of food in the refrigerator, so you can invite some friends for lunch," she said.

Suddenly Carol did not feel at all like laughing. The twins' friends would have to come for lunch. Carol had not seen much of the girls these last few days. When she met them in the street they talked to her, but they did not invite her to their homes and they did not come to see her. Christine had been angry because Carol had not come to the club meeting at her home, and Ruth had been hurt when Carol practically told her not to walk to the library with her. Now Betsy was annoyed because Carol had not gone to her house the day of the prize giving at the library.

Carol felt better when she saw how lovingly Daddy looked at her. "With you taking charge, we won't worry about a thing," he said. The way he said it made Carol feel grown up and important. She promised herself that she would take good care of everything, especially of the twins, even though they did not want to be taken care of.

The next morning Mother and Daddy left early. A little before eleven o'clock Carol started for the library with the twins, who were going to story hour. About a block from the library, they met Tim and his mother going toward the subway.

"We're going to the Central Park Zoo," Tim said. "Want to come with us?"

"You bet," Johnny told him. "We've been wanting to go ever since we moved to New York." He and Jinny had turned around and were ready to go with Tim when Carol stopped them. They would have to wait for another time, she said. She and Mother had talked over how they would spend the day, and Carol did not want them to do anything that Mother did not know about.

"But there's a great big new tiger in the zoo," Johnny said. "Don't you want to see him?"

"Some other time," Carol insisted. The twins glared at her.

On the upper floor of the library, a group of small boys and girls were already seated, waiting for the librarian to start telling a story. Carol told the twins that she would meet them right there at twelve o'clock.

"Honestly, you don't have to come back and get us," Jinny told her. "We know the way home as well as you do."

Carol knew that this was true, but today of all days nothing must go wrong. What if the twins were run over on their way home from the library! They never looked where they were going. What if they were kidnaped! Carol would never forgive herself. She seemed to hear Daddy's quiet voice saying, "With you taking charge, we won't worry about a thing."

Carol looked at the fiction shelves, chose two books for herself, had them stamped at the librarian's desk, and went out of the building. She left an order at the grocery store, then crossed the street and went upstairs. Just as she put her finger on the bell, she remembered that there was no one at home. For the first time in her life Carol opened the door with a key. It gave her a grown-up feeling that vanished the minute she stepped into the hall. No voice called, "Hello, Carol." The quiet seemed to rush at her the way the noise had during her first few days in New York. She hurried to the radio and clicked it on. There, it was nice to hear a voice, anyone's voice.

Soon the dumb-waiter bell rang and Carol hurried into the kitchen. She opened the dumb-waiter door. "All right," she called down the shaft. The ropes began to move. Soon the dumb-waiter shelf was in front of her and Carol removed the box of groceries that was on it. She put the box on the kitchen table. "All right," she called down again. The ropes moved again and the shelf descended.

By the time Carol had put the groceries away and read one or two chapters of her new book, it was time to call for the twins. She arrived at the library just as a group of children came rushing out. The twins were not among them. "Good," thought Carol, "they're waiting upstairs, just the way I told them to." Somehow, she had not expected the twins to be so obedient.

Carol walked up the stairs into the children's room. Story hour was over, but there were still a few boys and girls in the room. Carol did not see the twins. It would be just like them, she thought, to hide behind one of the bookracks or in a corner and then, when Carol passed, to jump out and say "Boo!" or something just as silly. She looked all around the room. She could not see the twins and began to feel a little worried. Maybe the librarian would know where Jinny and Johnny had gone. Somehow, no one ever had any trouble remembering the twins.

The librarian remembered Jinny and Johnny all too well, and she frowned the minute Carol said "twins." They had been in such a hurry to leave, she said sternly, that they rushed out during the first story. They had knocked over a chair in their haste.

Carol thanked her and told herself there was nothing to worry about. The twins had been bored, and they never liked to sit still. Most likely she would find them playing right on this block.

But the twins were not outside the library nor on either side of the street. Carol turned the corner and continued walking. She tried to look at both sides of the street at once. She stopped and talked to boys and girls who knew Jinny and Johnny, but no one had met them that morning.

The sun was very hot now. It beat down on Carol's head. Her hands were damp. She found herself taking out her handkerchief, mopping her face with it, putting the handkerchief back, taking it out again. The small handkerchief was soon very wet.

Once, as Carol walked along, she heard a woman shouting from a top-floor apartment, "Alice, come right up for lunch!" That gave Carol an idea. Wherever the twins were, they would surely be home for lunch. Probably right this very minute they were waiting impatiently for her in front of their own building. They couldn't get into the apartment because Carol had the key. Well, serves them right. Carol decided that she would walk very slowly and keep them waiting. While she told herself that, she rushed as fast as she could.

The twins were not outside the building.

"I bet they climbed the fire escape somehow and got in," Carol told herself. "I left the window open. They want to climb that fire escape almost as much as they want to ride up on the dumb-waiter."

She ran upstairs so quickly that she was panting when she reached the fourth floor. For the second time that day she put the key into the keyhole, but this time her fingers trembled so that she could hardly find the hole. For the second time she entered an empty, lonely apartment. Again the silence seemed louder than any of the New York noises.

Carol threw herself into the big chair and wondered what to do next.

Maybe the twins had dropped into the shoe-repair shop, and maybe they had told Frank, or his father or uncle, where they were going. Carol did not really think so, but anything was worth trying.

Frank was not in the store. His father and uncle smiled at Carol when she entered. Uncle Angelo explained in broken English that Frank was out on an errand. Carol looked worried. Uncle Angelo asked if he could help.

Glad to talk to anyone about her problem, Carol told him about the twins. Had he seen them? Had they dropped into the store and told him where they were going?

Uncle Angelo made sympathetic, clicking sounds with his tongue, but he shook his head from side to side as Carol talked. No, the twins had not been in the store all morning. He turned and talked to Frank's father in rapid Italian. Frank's father looked thoughtful. For a minute he did not say anything, then he too began to talk quickly in Italian. Uncle Angelo listened and nodded.

"My brother wishes to know, was there some place special the children wanted to go? Maybe they went there. You know how children are."

The moment Uncle Angelo said that, Carol knew just where the twins were. At least she knew where they had started for. Why hadn't she thought of that right away? Ever since they had lived in New York, Johnny and Jinny had wanted to visit the Central Park Zoo. Just this very morning they had wanted to go there with Tim and his mother.

Where, though, was the zoo? How would she find it? How in the world had the twins found it? By now Carol knew that Central Park extended for miles and miles, and the zoo was nowhere near the bandstand where Pat had won his freckle prize.

Neither Frank's father nor his uncle could tell her how to get to the zoo. If only Frank or Maria were at home, they might know.

Carol felt more worried than ever as she went out into the hot sunlight. She was sure that the twins had not found their way to the zoo. Never had she felt so helpless.

As she stood outside the shoe-repair shop wondering what to do next, a loud, shrill noise came directly toward her. It was really a combination of sounds — the loud, thin, shrieking of a whistle and at the same time the clang, clang, clang of a bell and the roar of one fire engine after another dashing past. The whistles grew louder, shriller, and more terrifying. The clang, clang, clang of the bells seemed more deafening. Even after the engines had passed and were on the next block, Carol could still hear the shrieking sounds.

The frightening sounds and the sight of the fire engines made Carol feel almost sick with worry. Right now the twins might be lying unconscious on some New York street, run over by big, shrieking, speeding fire engines. She could picture a crowd around the two small figures. No one would know who they were. How could Carol face Mother and Father when they came home tonight? They had trusted her, and they would never trust her again.

"I can't just stand here," Carol thought. "I've got to do something. I've got to get someone to help me. I'll ask Ruth." The thought of Ruth's smiling, friendly face made Carol feel less frightened.

Carol rang Ruth's bell. She put her finger on it and pressed it for several seconds, but no one answered.

"I'll ask Betsy to help me," Carol thought. Betsy had made it rather plain that she did not like Carol. She might not even want to help, but Carol made up her mind to ask her anyway. There were times when you needed friends.

Chapter 9

The Search

WHEN Betsy opened the door, there was a friendly smile on her face. It faded when she saw Carol standing there. "Hello," she said, and that was all. She did not ask Carol to come in.

Standing in the hall, Carol heard familiar voices and the sound of laughter. Now she felt more miserable than ever. Mixed with her worry about the twins was envy of these girls who were such good friends and who always had so much to talk and laugh about. It did not make Carol feel any happier to remember what Mother had said. The girls had been friendly to her when she first moved to New York. She could have been a member of their group by now.

Standing at the open door, Carol told Betsy about the twins. Her voice trembled. "I don't even know how to get to the zoo," she said. "I thought maybe you'd know and you'd tell me."

As Carol talked, she saw Betsy's expression change from cool politeness to concern.

"I don't know how to get to the zoo either, but I'll find out," Betsy said. "Gosh, I wouldn't want anything to happen to the twins. Come on in."

In the living room, Maria, Christine, and Ruth sat in comfortable chairs, eating strawberry ice cream and sponge cake. On the table in the center of the room another dish of pink ice cream was rapidly melting.

The girls seemed embarrassed when Carol came into the room. "Want some of my ice cream? I've got plenty," Ruth said.

"Who knows how to get to the Central Park Zoo?" Betsy asked before Carol could answer. The girls looked at Betsy and Carol in surprise. Their expressions, too, changed to concern when Betsy told them what had happened. "It's not polite to leave my guests, but I think I'll go with Carol," Betsy said. "She's not a New Yorker, and she could easily get lost."

None of the girls knew just how to get to the Central Park Zoo. They had all been there at one time or another with their parents or their classes, but they did not remember just how they had gone.

"Pat will know. He knows how to get everywhere," Maria suggested. Then she added in a lower voice, "Nothing must happen to the twins."

Ruth said that Pat was at the garage, helping the owner. If it were any day but Saturday he would probably go with Carol, but on Saturday he got most of his tips.

As Carol and Betsy turned to go, Christine asked them if they had money for subway fare. Carol was just about to say, "Of course," when she remembered something. The last time she had rushed into the apartment to see if the twins were home for lunch she had dropped her pocketbook on a chair. Then she had rushed out of the house without picking it up. The door locked itself without a key, and not until this minute had Carol realized that she did not have her purse with her. Her face grew red. It was bad enough to ask for help without borrowing money too. She explained to the girls.

"I can lend you ten cents," Maria said, taking two nickels out of her dress pocket.

"I have ten cents I was going to buy buns with," Ruth added. Christine had a nickel, and she gave that to Carol. Then Betsy remembered a little pitcher in the kitchen. Her mother kept small change in it. Betsy took all the change.

Carol thanked them for helping her.

"It's okay," Christine answered. "We'd do anything for the twins. We're all crazy about them."

Carol did not know whether she imagined it or whether each time the girls said they were crazy about the twins, they emphasized the two words *the twins*. Now it seemed to her that Christine also emphasized the word *them*. There was no question in Carol's mind that the girls wanted to help the twins, not her.

Pat was putting gasoline into the tank of a big blue car when Carol and Betsy reached the garage. He was so busy that he hardly looked up. "Be with you girls in a second," he said. It seemed more like hours to Carol, who shifted from one foot to the other, wishing that Pat would hurry. The gasoline overflowed onto the garage floor. The heavy, sweet odor filled the garage and Carol found herself covering her nose.

After Pat had put the gasoline into the tank and put back the hose, he cleaned the windshield of the car, raised the hood to see if there was enough water, decided there was not, went to the back of the garage, and returned with a can of water. Carol was so worried by this time that she felt like knocking the can out of Pat's hand. Then Pat took the man's money, gave it to the owner of the garage, waited for change, returned the change to the man, took the tip the man gave him, and put it in his pocket. The man drove away.

Pat turned to the girls. "Anything I can do for you?" he asked.

Carol was so nervous she let Betsy tell the story.

"Sure I can tell you how to get to the zoo," Pat said. He started to explain.

To Carol, his directions did not mean a thing, so she looked at Betsy. Betsy looked puzzled too. "Let's start over again," she said to Pat. "We go down to the subway. We take a local, not an express, and then . . . ?"

Pat turned up his freckled nose. "Gosh, you'll never get there," he said. "We'll have to look for four people instead of two. I'll tell the boss I'm going with you. Wait a second." He rushed to the back of the garage. In a second he had returned. "I didn't even wait to wash my hands. Smell," he said, putting his hands right in front of Carol's nose. She stepped back in disgust. His hands were greasy and smelled of gasoline. Wasn't it just like Pat to be so impolite, she thought.

"Isn't it just like Pat to give up tips and come with us?" Betsy asked in a low voice.

On the way to the subway station Pat kept saying that the twins were perfectly safe and that they could find their way anywhere. Carol wished that she felt as sure. The twins did not know anything about New York. How could they ever find their way to the zoo?

They had just reached the subway when they heard voices calling their names. Maria, Ruth, Christine, and Frank rushed toward them. They were breathless and panting from running.

"We decided we'd better all go," Maria said. "There are so many places to look, the more of us the better."

So many places! Carol had thought that the zoo was a very small section of Central Park and that all the animals were in one place. Now the whole trip seemed useless. They would never find the twins. Probably Jinny and Johnny had not even reached the park. Maybe they had boarded the wrong train and gone to Brooklyn or some other place so far away that they would never be able to find their way home.

As they walked down the steps into the subway station, Carol heard a loud roar.

"There's a train. Maybe if we run we can make it," Pat shouted. He rushed down the steps to the change booth, with the others close behind him. As they put their tokens in the turnstiles, they saw the train start to pull away.

"Now we'll have to wait for the next one," Pat said. He walked calmly over to a slot machine, put in a penny, punched a lever, and was soon busily chewing a stick of gum.

Carol almost burst out crying. Everything seemed to be against her. Nervously she walked to the edge of the platform and looked down the tracks to see if there was another train coming. It was like looking down a long, dark tunnel lighted dimly here and there by electric lights. No, there was no train coming. Carol stepped back.

"In another minute," Frank said quietly. Carol could not stand still. Again she looked down the tracks, and this time she saw two small white lights far off in the distance. The lights grew larger as they came toward her. Then she jumped back as a long train of cars roared into the station. The first few cars sped past and then the train stopped. The doors slid open. Pat walked in first and the others followed and found seats. The doors closed. The train started, jerked, then sped on its way.

This was the first time that Carol had ever been in a subway train, but she was too worried to be interested. Now that she was really in the train she felt more frightened than ever. When she closed her eyes, she could picture Johnny walking to the edge of the platform and leaning forward as she had done. She could picture him losing his balance and falling onto the tracks just as a train rushed into the station. Although there was a large electric fan whirring right over Carol's head, the perspiration rolled down her face.

The subway trip really took less than fifteen minutes, but to her it seemed hours. Why didn't the train go faster, she kept asking herself. She clenched her fist at each station when the doors opened and people took their time walking in and out of the car. When someone held the door open so that a man rushing down the steps could get in, Carol wanted to scream.

The worst part was that this train did not take them directly to the zoo, as she had thought it would. After they had gone from the dark subway station up into the bright sunlight, they had to walk quite a distance through Central Park. Carol heard the others talking and laughing, but she was too upset to listen to what they were saying. The trip seemed more and more useless. How could Jinny and Johnny possibly have found their way? How did anyone in New York ever find his way around this tremendous city? Carol was sure that she never would.

They passed many people in the park, sitting on benches, lying on the grass, and walking around. Soon Carol found that they were in a particularly crowded section. Here there were more children than in the other part of the park. They all seemed very happy. Some were sucking lollipops. Some were eating Good Humors; some, hot dogs. Some were drinking bottles of soda pop. There were children shouting, jumping rope, riding bicycles, and playing ball. Carol, who wanted to rush straight to the tiger cage, found herself walking slowly, so that she would not bump into any of the children.

This section of Central Park did not smell as fresh and clean as the rest of it. Soon Carol discovered the reason. Ahead of her were rows of cages, with one animal in each cage. Farther on were stone buildings.

"Well, we're in the zoo," Pat said. "Let's divide. Ruthie, you look at the cages in this section. Christine, you go look over there. Betsy, you take that end. Carol, you go to the building over there. That's where the tigers are. Frankie, you go to the third house, and I'll just travel around. We'll meet over there, in front of the seals, in twenty minutes. Ready — set — go!"

Again Carol wanted to shake Pat, because he

looked as if he were enjoying himself. She rushed toward the building that Pat had pointed out to her. Just inside the door she stopped to catch her breath. The smell of animals was so strong that Carol closed her eyes and sneezed. Again and again she sneezed. While her eyes were closed, she told herself that when she opened them she would see Jinny and Johnny the very first thing. She opened her eyes slowly. The twins were nowhere in sight.

A guard came toward Carol, and she asked him where the tiger was. He pointed toward the middle of the room. Carol hurried to the cage. In front of it was a crowd of people, mostly boys and girls. She pushed her way through the crowd toward the front. She heard someone say, "Hey, where do you think you're going?" She did not care. The twins were not in front of the tiger's cage.

Very slowly Carol walked around the room. In front of each cage she pushed her way toward the front, as she had done at the tiger's cage. She did not look at the animals at all, just at the people. Once she found herself looking at the bars of the cage, wondering if a small boy could stick his head between those bars and be eaten by the animal.

After another visit to the tiger's cage Carol gave up. The twins were not in the building; that was certain. She was so tired and so discouraged that she wanted to throw herself on the grass and cry. Her collar was wet with perspiration, and her heart was pounding.

Ruth and Christine were already there when Carol walked over to where the seals were busily splashing around in their pool. Carol saw Betsy coming from the other direction. Their faces all looked worried and serious. Soon Frank joined them. No one had seen the twins. No one knew just where to go next or what to do.

Now Carol wished two things at once. She wished that Pat would stay away for a long time, so that she could still have hope. She wished, too, that he would hurry, so that she would know whether or not he had found Jinny and Johnny.

The second wish came true. Pat came toward them without the twins. He was whistling. "Didn't anyone find the kids?" he asked cheerfully, looking from one to the other.

Carol decided that Pat did not have any feelings at all. She was not surprised, but she was surprised when Frank, who had been so sympathetic, grinned from ear to ear.

"Pat, you are down to something. I can tell by your face," Frank said.

"You mean *up* to something," Maria corrected him. Then she too smiled, and so did the others.

Carol could not believe her eyes. Suddenly they all looked pleased, for no reason at all.

"Where are those twins?" Betsy demanded. "We're sure you found them."

Pat cupped his hands in front of his mouth. Then in the loudest voice that Carol had ever heard he shouted, "Okay, kids, come on out." Everyone who was passing looked at him. Carol blushed in embarrassment, but she felt happier than at any time since she had looked around the children's room at the library and realized that the twins were not there. How long ago that seemed!

Carol had not known whether she would hug the twins or shake them when they were found. Now, as they rushed out of nowhere, their eyes bright with excitement, she did not do either. She burst out crying. Everyone looked embarrassed.

Maria came over shyly and put her hand through Carol's arm. "What is it you say in America?" she asked. "All is well that ends well?"

"We didn't mean to worry you, honest we didn't," Jinny said when she saw Carol crying. "We thought we'd sneak out of the library, rush to the zoo, look at the tiger, and rush back before story hour was over."

"But it took longer to get here than we thought," Johnny interrupted. "And there were so many things to see. Golly, we haven't seen all the animals yet. We're coming back the first chance we get."

"But we'll tell you next time, so you won't worry," Jinny assured Carol, who felt very foolish now because she had cried.

On the way out of the park, the twins kept talking excitedly. "We spent all our money on Good Humors, and we forgot how to go home because we lost the directions. We didn't know what to do, and we were starving." When Johnny paused to catch his breath, Jinny continued. "We never heard a nicer sound than Pat's voice yelling our names. Gosh, were we glad to hear it!" Jinny looked up at Pat admiringly.

Pat's grin stretched from ear to ear. "I really can yell when I want to," he said modestly. "I went from place to place and yelled. I knew if they were anywhere around, they'd hear me—and they did." Carol had never thought that she would be thankful for Pat's loud voice.

The trip home seemed shorter than the trip down. When the train stopped at their station and all of them walked up to the street, Carol remembered something. She had not eaten her lunch. She turned to the others a little timidly. "Mother left lots of food in the refrigerator. She told me to invite my friends up for lunch. I wish you'd all come." Somehow it seemed very important to Carol that they should come.

But Pat had to get back to the garage. Ruth said she was sorry but she had to go home and start supper. Christine had to do some marketing. Betsy said she was sorry too, but she had to practice on her violin. Frank said that he was needed in the store, and Maria had told her mother she would go with her to pick out a present for Frank's mother's birthday.

Carol did not know whether the girls were telling the truth or making up stories because they did not want to be friendly. They had made it plain that they helped her only because they liked the twins so much. Carol felt the same ache that she had felt when she read Helen's letter.

"I wish you'd come," she said, "but if you can't, thanks for helping me find the twins. I don't know what I'd have done without you. I'll pay you the money I owe you as soon as Mother and Daddy get home." She was so tired and so disappointed that her voice trembled.

"Glad we could help," Christine said.

On the way upstairs Carol stopped. She remembered that she had left her pocketbook and key in the apartment.

"Yippee!" Johnny shouted. "Now I get to climb the fire escape. I'll go into Pat's apartment, climb down, and go through the window. Some day I'm going to take a dumb-waiter ride."

Later, when they were seated at the table eating, Carol asked the twins how they had ever found their way to the park. Johnny and Jinny looked at each other and grinned. Johnny explained. A short time after they had moved to New York, they had asked the man in the change booth of the subway station how to get to the zoo. They really had thought that they would go with Mother and Carol, or, if it were on a Sunday, with Daddy too. Well, they couldn't remember what the man said, so they asked him to write it down carefully. The man even drew a map, showing them where to walk after they got out of the subway station.

"We couldn't make head or tail of the map, so we asked people," Jinny said. "Everyone was nice. They helped us cross Columbus Circle, and one man bought us some popcorn. We didn't have any trouble."

"It sure was a wonderful day," Johnny added. "It musta been nice for Mrs. Pain-in-the-neck too. No one was home all day."

Chapter 10

Miss Tyler Doesn't Knock

THAT EVENING Mother and Daddy listened attentively while Jinny and Johnny told about their adventures, and then while Carol told about hers. Carol watched her parents' expressions change as they listened. First they looked troubled, then really worried, then relieved.

"Well, just as long as you got home safely we won't start worrying now," Daddy said.

"There wasn't anything to worry about really," Jinny explained. "We had the most wonderful day in all our life. I'm going to write to Linda about it tomorrow. She could never get lost back in the country the way we did."

Linda had been Jinny's best friend, just as Helen

had been Carol's. Hearing Jinny talk about writing reminded Carol that she had not answered Helen's letter yet. There still was nothing that she wanted to write about. She sighed.

"Anything wrong?" Mother asked.

"I suppose you'll never trust us alone again," Carol said. It was really more like a question.

"Nonsense," Mother answered. "I'm going downtown to do Red Cross work Wednesday morning. So next Wednesday you'll be on your own again."

Carol felt happier. Mother and Daddy had not scolded or thought that anything had been Carol's fault. When Daddy gave her the money to pay back to the others, he advised her not to do it until the next day. "They'll trust you," he said. "They're nice kids all right, aren't they?"

Carol said, "Yes, they are," without hesitating. She meant it too.

Mother said that Carol looked tired and should go to bed early. Carol was glad to obey. She felt more tired than if she had worked hard all day. Although she went to bed early, she could not seem to fall asleep. Sentences kept popping into her mind. She wished that her mind had a little knob like the radio, and she could turn it off and not hear voices. She seemed to hear the girls saying over and over again: "We're crazy about the *twins*. We wouldn't want anything to happen to the *twins*. No, we're sorry but we can't come upstairs." She seemed to hear Mother's voice saying something it had said many days ago: "You have no talent for friendship," and "What an unhappy, friendless woman Miss Tyler must be!"

When Carol fell asleep, she dreamed that it was the first day of school. Boys and girls were walking in groups behind her and ahead of her. Carol, all by herself, walked between them. They shouted back and forth to one another as if they did not see her.

Carol felt someone shaking her. "Stop groaning and stop talking about school," Jinny said. "It's bad enough that it has to start in September without you talking about it now."

On Wednesday morning Mother had to wear her rubbers and carry her umbrella, for the day was dark and sunless. The rain came down steadily. It was the kind of day when you did not know what to do. Carol practiced, read, and drew. She thought of writing to Helen, but she felt too lazy.

While Carol was reading, the twins decided to play a duet. The idea was to see who could play the loudest. Neither Jinny nor Johnny could read notes. They put their hands down on the piano keys and banged. The noise was so loud and so unpleasant that Carol put her hands over her ears. Mrs. Pain-in-the-neck would be furious.

"You'd better stop before Mrs. Pain-in-the-neck knocks," she told the twins. How was it that she hadn't knocked before now? Carol wondered.

"She's out, or we'd have heard from her by now," Johnny said, and he banged louder than ever.

Carol remembered what Miss Tyler had told her the day that she brought the letter. Miss Tyler had said that she must have quiet on rainy days because her sinus bothered her and she never went out in the rain.

The twins kept banging and Carol kept waiting for the knock-knock-knock of Mrs. Pain-in-the-neck's broom. She was beginning to worry. Something must be wrong if she was not complaining.

Carol stood up. She really did not know what she was going to say until she said it. "I'm going downstairs and see if Miss Tyler is all right."

Jinny and Johnny opened their gray eyes very wide and looked at Carol in amazement.

"She hasn't knocked, so she must be sick," Carol explained, and walked out of the apartment before the twins could say a word.

Carol walked down the flight of stairs. In front of

Miss Tyler's door she hesitated. What would she do if Mrs. Pain-in-the-neck, tall and fierce, opened the door and said, "What do you want?" It would not be polite to say, "I thought you were sick or something because you weren't complaining."

"I really am crazy," Carol told herself. "I ought to go right back upstairs." As she said it, she put her finger on the bell and rang it gently. She waited, listening. There was no sound from within.

She turned to go upstairs, hesitated, and came back. This time she rang the bell loudly. Again she waited. There were no footsteps coming down the hallway. No harsh voice said, "Who is there?" There was no clanking of the chain that locked Miss Tyler's door.

For a second Carol stood still. Then she knelt down and put her ear against the keyhole. Was that a sound, or did she imagine it? She pressed her ear even closer to the keyhole. She held her breath. As she listened, it started again. It sounded for a minute as if someone were moaning. Then there was complete silence, not a sound from inside.

Carol jumped up, her knees trembling. She rushed upstairs.

"Was she there?" Johnny asked.

"No one answered the doorbell," Carol said, "but

I'm frightened." She decided not to tell the twins about the sound she had heard. "Johnny, will you climb down the fire escape and look in Miss Tyler's window and see if you see any sign of her inside?"

"Yippee!" Johnny shouted. "Will I climb down the fire escape!" He put on his coat and rain hat and climbed out of the window.

"Be very careful," Carol told him. "The steps are slippery."

She and Jinny watched him go carefully from one slippery step to another. They saw him stop in front of Miss Tyler's window.

Carol saw her brother look into the window downstairs. Then, instead of climbing back up, he continued to climb down. What in the world could he be thinking of? The fire escape went down only as far as the first floor, not to the street. It was too high for anyone to jump down, except in an emergency. Carol held her breath as she watched Johnny; then he disappeared.

"Where did he go?" Carol said.

Jinny giggled. "Pete lives on the first floor. I guess he went in to visit him."

A few minutes later the dumb-waiter bell rang. "Who in the world is that?" Carol wondered out loud. "We don't expect any groceries."

"I guess it's Johnny telling us about Mrs. Pain-in-the-neck," Jinny explained, as if it were perfectly natural for Johnny to talk to his sisters through the dumb-waiter instead of coming upstairs.

Carol opened the dumb-waiter door and called hello.

"Hey, Carol, her shade's pulled down and I couldn't see anything," Johnny shouted. "I knocked on the window and nobody came. Hey, Carol, I'm getting worried about her too."

"Did you ask Mr. Swensen if he saw her?" Carol asked. "Maybe he could get into the apartment and look."

"The Swensens aren't home," Johnny called back. "I thought of that too, and I knocked at their door. No one's home."

Johnny, down in the basement, started to pull at one of the dumb-waiter ropes. Carol saw it wriggle. It gave her an idea.

"Johnny, come right up as fast as you can," she shouted in a voice that was almost as loud as her brother's.

Johnny was upstairs so soon it seemed as if he must have flown up. He was panting when he came into the kitchen.

"Could you stand on the dumb-waiter?" Carol

asked him. "Jinny and I will pull you down as far as Miss Tyler's. See if you can open her dumb-waiter door and get in. I'm sure there's something wrong."

"Don't you do it!" Jinny shrieked. "She'll think you're a burglar and she'll shoot you. Don't you do it."

Johnny acted as if he hadn't heard his twin. "Yip-pee!" he shouted. "I always wanted to take a dumb-waiter ride." He pulled at the rope until the top shelf was a little below the open door. Then he climbed onto it as if he were climbing out of a win-dow onto a ledge. He stood erect and held on to one of the ropes.

Carol began to pull. She pulled and pulled, but the dumb-waiter did not move. She pulled until the palms of her hands were red. Finally the dumb-waiter began to move.

"I'm heavier than a box of groceries or a garbage pail," Johnny said proudly. "They're easy to pull up and down."

By the time Johnny reached Miss Tyler's dumb-waiter door, Carol's hands were stiff and sore. It was a relief to take them off the thick ropes.

Carol could hear Johnny banging against Miss Tyler's dumb-waiter door. "Okay, I've got it open,"

he called. "Here I go." A minute later a voice that did not sound at all like Johnny's said, "She's on the floor in the living room. She doesn't move. What'll I do?" Carol had never heard her brother's voice sound so frightened.

She tried to keep her own voice as calm as possible. "Open the hall door so I can get in," she said. "I'll be right down."

Johnny had taken the chain off Miss Tyler's door and was waiting when Carol got there. He was very pale. "She's on the floor," he said again, "all stretched out on the floor."

Miss Tyler lay there with her eyes closed. Her face was white, and once in a while she moaned. Near her was a chair that had fallen backward. A broom lay on the floor. Carol realized what must have happened. Miss Tyler must have wanted to knock on the ceiling when the twins were banging on the piano. She must have been climbing up on the chair with the broom in her hand when she lost her balance and fell.

"Let's put her in bed," Johnny suggested. "We can't leave her here on the floor."

All at once Carol remembered the silly rhyme that the twins had made up: "We won't do one thing more — we'll leave her on the floor." She remembered what Mother had said. Mother had told them never to move anyone who had fallen, but to leave the person just where he or she was.

"Let's not touch her," Carol said. "You get Dr. Warren. You know where Betsy lives, don't you? Tell her father what happened, and tell him to come right over. I'll stay here."

When Johnny had gone, Carol wet her handkerchief at the kitchen sink and put it on Miss Tyler's forehead. "The doctor's coming soon, and he'll take care of you," she said. Her voice sounded like Mother's when she or the twins were sick. Carol wished Mother were here now. Mother would know what to do. If only Johnny and the doctor would hurry!

Carol was still bathing Miss Tyler's forehead when Dr. Warren and Johnny came in. The doctor knelt on the floor. He touched Miss Tyler's leg. She groaned and opened her eyes. Carol shivered as if she herself were feeling the pain.

"Broken leg," Dr. Warren said. "Is there anyone who can come and take care of you, Miss Tyler, or would you rather go to the hospital?"

"Hospital," Miss Tyler whispered. "No family. No friends." Then she fainted.

The small kitchen seemed crowded and airless. Carol felt as if she were suffocating, but it was not entirely from the heat. She felt sorrier for Miss Tyler than she had ever felt for anyone in her whole life. No family and no friends. Carol looked down at her. Her eyes were open again and she was biting her lips in pain. "We're your friends, Miss Tyler," she said. She could hardly believe that it was she who had said it.

Dr. Warren put his hand on her shoulder. "You handled this very well, Carol," he said. "You were calm and efficient. I'm very proud that you're a friend of Betsy's."

The doctor's praise made Carol feel proud too.

By the time Miss Tyler was brought downstairs on a stretcher and carried to the ambulance, a crowd had collected outside the building. Everyone was asking questions and talking about what had happened. They stretched their necks to see Miss Tyler.

Johnny rushed into the middle of the crowd. "That's my sister! That's Carol!" he shouted when Carol came down the steps. "She told me to go down there. We saved her life!"

Carol felt herself blushing as the people stared at her. "Hurray for Carol!" a man shouted. Someone else called, "Good work, girl!" Someone else clapped, and soon everyone was clapping. Carol turned around and ran upstairs.

They had clapped for her! She had pictured girls and boys clapping for her after she won the art prize. Instead, men and women she didn't know had clapped because she had helped Miss Tyler. Helping a person was more important, Carol suddenly thought, than winning a prize.

Johnny and Jinny came in. "Know what Miss Tyler said to me?" Johnny asked. "I leaned over to say 'So long,' and she winked at me and said while she was in the hospital we could jump up and down all we wanted, but we had to keep quiet when she got home."

Chapter 11

Carol's Friends

AT NOON, Mother hurried into the apartment. "Carol, I heard all about it," she said excitedly. "Everyone stopped and told me. Oh darling, I'm so proud of you."

A few minutes later a key turned in the door. The door opened and slammed shut. Daddy, always so quiet and slow in his movements, dashed into the kitchen. "Carol, everyone's talking about the way you saved Miss Tyler. You were wonderful."

"We're the most popular family on the block," Jinny told Daddy proudly. "I'm proudest of Johnny, though. He did the hard work, standing on the dumb-waiter and getting into Mrs. Pain . . . I mean Miss Tyler's apartment." Jinny seemed to have forgotten that she had begged Johnny not to do it.

"Mother and I are proud of both of you," Daddy said. "Now I'm sure you'd all like a quiet lunch after all the excitement."

As soon as they were seated around the kitchen table, the bell rang. Jinny rushed to open the door. "Hi, Pat," they heard her say.

"Out of my way, kid," Pat told her. "I gotta see Carrie." Somehow the way he said it made Carol smile instead of being angry.

Pat drew up a chair and helped himself to some bread and jelly. "You were swell, Carrie," he said. "Who'd ever have thought about Mrs. Pain-in-the-neck? I wouldn't, but I'm awfully glad you did. Who's that?"

The bell had rung again. "Did you say something about a nice quiet lunch?" Mother asked Daddy, smiling.

"That's what happens when you have a heroine in the family," Daddy said. His eyes, like Mother's, glowed with happiness.

Betsy came into the kitchen. She didn't seem to see anyone in the room but Carol. "Daddy told me about it," she said. "Daddy said that Miss Tyler could have been on the floor for days, and no one would have known. He said it's because you were thoughtful and calm that she'll be all right. He said he's proud you're a friend of mine."

You're a friend of mine. Those were just the words that Carol had hoped to hear Betsy say; then she had given up hoping. The more she knew Betsy, the more she wanted her for a friend. It was not because she was richer than the others or wore prettier dresses or because her father was a doctor. It was because Betsy did not care about any of these things. Betsy liked you for what you were, and when she was your friend she was a real friend. Carol, remembering that day in the park when she had talked about Ruth, blushed.

Again the bell rang. This was like the day after the Clarks had moved into this apartment. On that day the sound of the bell had annoyed Carol. Now she was eager to know who was there.

Ruth and Christine joined the others. Ruth threw her arms around Carol and hugged her. "I'm so proud we're friends," she said. Christine, who stood stiffly beside Ruth, said, "Me too."

When the bell rang again, Frank and Maria came in. "It's like a movie," Maria said.

"And Carol is the beautiful star," Frank added. At the word *beautiful,* Carol blushed and smiled.

Pat said, "Gosh, Carrie's got a dimple. I never noticed it before." Carol realized why he hadn't. She had not smiled very often since they moved to New York.

"Carol's the heroine, but I'm the hero," Johnny reminded them.

Christine interrupted. "Say, Carol, remember when I asked you if you wanted to go to Coney Island next time we went? Well, we're going next Saturday if the weather's nice. Want to come?"

Carol said that she would love to.

"Take us too! Take us!" Jinny urged. She and Johnny began to jump up and down. Then they looked at each other and stopped. "We can't make any noise when she's in the hospital," Jinny said sadly.

"But she told us we could till she gets home," Johnny reminded her. "I don't feel like jumping either, though, with her sick. We'll just have to wait till she comes back."

Mother suggested that they all have lemonade and cookies. Carol, surrounded by her friends, felt really happy for the first time since the Clarks had moved to New York. Now she could answer Helen's letter. She would answer it this very evening. She would tell Helen that she had made many friends in New York, that she had helped a neighbor, and that although she had not done anything special, everyone seemed to think she was a heroine. She would mention that six of her new friends — two of them boys — had dropped in during the afternoon for a visit. She would tell Helen that next Saturday she and the girls were going swimming in the ocean. She would invite Helen to come to New York before long and meet her new friends.

Betsy's voice interrupted Carol's thoughts. "I wish he'd stop," said Betsy. Carol realized that someone outside was honking his horn, and she had not even noticed it. A bus rumbled by. A child's voice shouted, "Get the ball, get the ball!" A loud, shrill whistle blew.

"Fire! Fire! Maybe it's this house," Johnny yelled. He rushed to the window. The noise was dying out in the distance. "No, it's not here," Johnny said in a disappointed voice. "Maybe next time it will be."

Carol's mind went back to the letter she was going to write to Helen. "If I ever go to visit Helen," she thought, "everything will seem so quiet. I'm not sure I'll like it."